Niall suspecte
of a foot fetish

"Come, Gigi," Niall called the dog.

Gigi ignored him, squeezing beneath the fencing and launching herself across the neighboring yard like a seven-pound rocket. Just as Niall reached the fence line, Gigi attacked the pair of bare toes hanging over a chaise lounge. The woman screamed and leaped to her feet.

In an instant, Niall's world tilted on its axis. His neighbor was heart-stopping, blood-pumping naked. He struggled to focus on the woman's face. It was damn hard.

"Let me guess—you're my new neighbor and *this* belongs to you." She nodded toward Gigi. Her distinctly Southern drawl held more than a note of amusement.

"Uh, yeah. I'm sorry we…uh…interrupted you."

"No problem—I didn't want to burn anyway." Her friendly smile was faintly provocative.

Although totally nude, the woman was calm, cool and collected. He, on the other hand, couldn't put together a cohesive sentence.

But he *did* know that he liked the neighborhood already….

Dear Reader,

I first met Tammy Cooper when I wrote my first Temptation novel, *Barely Mistaken*. Tammy, the heroine's sister, was a bad girl—bad attitude, bad track record, bad reputation. But the more I got to know Tammy, the more I realized she wasn't all that bad, just misunderstood. It's trite, but true. Beneath the rebellious facade beat the heart of a vulnerable woman who deserved to be happy—even if she didn't think so.

That's the beauty of writing for Temptation—I got to give Tammy her own happy ending. But not just any man would do. Tammy had already tried that, and it didn't work. No, Tammy needed a man who would delve deep enough to discover the true woman who hid behind the reputation. And lucky for her, that man moved in just next door....

Things heat up pretty quickly between them, and they learn two valuable lessons. One, that Tammy's not as bad as she pretends, and two—that Niall is even *better* than he looks.... I hope you enjoy *Barely Behaving*. I'd love to hear from you. You can write to me at P.O. Box 801068, Acworth, GA 30101.

Happy reading,

Jennifer LaBrecque

Books by Jennifer LaBrecque

HARLEQUIN TEMPTATION
886—BARELY MISTAKEN
904—BARELY DECENT

HARLEQUIN DUETS
28—ANDREW IN EXCESS
52—KIDS+COPS=CHAOS
64—JINGLE BELL BRIDE

JENNIFER LABRECQUE

BARELY BEHAVING

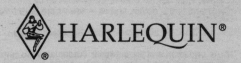

HARLEQUIN®

TORONTO • NEW YORK • LONDON
AMSTERDAM • PARIS • SYDNEY • HAMBURG
STOCKHOLM • ATHENS • TOKYO • MILAN • MADRID
PRAGUE • WARSAW • BUDAPEST • AUCKLAND

To Jake, forever in our hearts, Advantage and Cleopatra
(formerly known as Fair Game). Also to Catherine McGovern
and Southeastern Greyhound Adoption (SEGA) for their
tireless dedication to saving these magnificent animals.

Special thanks to Julie Lugar, DVM, for her friendship, extraordinary
veterinary skills and her patience with all my questions.
Any misinformation or inconsistencies
are strictly my own ineptness.

RECYCLED PAPER · RECYCLED PAPER

ISBN 0-373-69152-1

BARELY BEHAVING

Copyright © 2003 by Jennifer LaBrecque.

Prologue

"SEX, MARRIAGE AND MEN don't mix. I like sex and I like men. But I'm skipping marriage from here on out. And this time I mean it."

Tammy Lorelei Cooper Williams Schill Brantley tossed her latest divorce decree onto her kitchen's tiled island. The papers skidded past the miniature tabletop Christmas tree toward her younger sister, Olivia. "And I'm taking back my maiden name. I'm going back to Cooper. I've finally figured out who I am." And by God, she liked the woman she'd come to know.

"I wish you'd let me kick your ex-husbands' no-good cheating butts." Olivia's gray eyes held a bloodthirsty glint.

Tammy laughed and shook her head as she scooped ice into the blender. Her quiet, conservative little sister had a whole other side. Especially now that Olivia was nine weeks pregnant. With her wildly fluctuating hormones, Olivia could shift from butt-kicking mad to uncontrollably weepy in sixty seconds.

"I appreciate the sentiment and I've thought about doing it myself a few times, but they're not worth it. Men are all pretty much the same when you come right down to it. They're made that way. Which means they'll take good sex any way they can get it. Even mediocre sex. Hey, just make that readily available sex."

Or at least that seemed to be the case with her ex-husbands. Tammy dressed sexy and she was an admitted flirt, but she'd taken her wedding vows seriously—she didn't fool around when she was married and she didn't fool around with someone else's spouse. Unfortunately, her ex-husbands hadn't shared her outlook.

She poured cranberry juice in the blender and tossed in pineapple chunks and a banana. She topped it off with a vitamin and soy packet.

Olivia pulled out two glasses from the cabinet. "Not all men are that way. You married good old boys who thought you should wait at home while they played the field."

Not pretty, but apropos. "That about sums up Jerry, Allen and Earl."

"But they're not all like that. You just haven't met the right man yet," Olivia said.

Tammy shook her head. Newlyweds. They always wanted to share the love.

"Personally, I don't believe in Mr. Right. But I wouldn't mind a round or two with Mr. Right Now. A year without sex—" Olivia checked her with a raised brow. "Okay. If I *have* to count the attempted reconciliation quickie with Earl—and I shouldn't have to because it wasn't very good—then it's been ten and a half months. But as of today, I'm no longer a married woman, so when Mr. Right Now comes along, watch out. It's been so bad lately I'm afraid to be left alone in the produce section." And she was only partly kidding. Ten and a half months was a long time.

During her separation, she'd been seriously tempted by two men. Earl's sister's husband, Tim, was a hottie. Tim had stroked her ego at a time she desperately needed it and offered to stroke other things. Lowell Evans, the town hunk, had also offered his own brand of solace. Hard as it'd been, she'd turned them both down.

"You can talk about Mr. Right Now, but I think you're an incurable romantic beneath all that cynicism." Speculation underlaid Olivia's laugher.

"Nope. Wrong on both counts. I'm a reformed romantic who's evolved into a realist." It was almost embarrassing to recall her naive certainty at seventeen that she and Jerry would love one another forever. That had died a swift but painful death when she'd caught him boinking Lilly Lawson. She'd *hoped* for love 'til death do us part when she'd married Allen. By the time she'd married Earl—she wasn't proud to admit it, even to herself—there'd been a hint of desperation in her pursuit of true love. "After three matrimonial rounds, I've figured out men consider fidelity a mutual fund investment."

Olivia uttered a compound obscenity Tammy'd never heard her use before. Actually, she didn't think Olivia knew words like that.

"Did you learn that from Luke?" It was still mind-blowing Olivia had married a rebel like Luke Rutledge instead of Luke's straight-arrow brother, whom she'd dated. Almost as strange as Tammy and Olivia becoming close friends and confidantes after thirty years of uneasy sisterhood.

Olivia smirked and pushed her tortoiseshell glasses more firmly on her nose. "No. I already knew it. But he does encourage me to use it."

"Well, don't get all wigged out about my exes. The way I see it, they did me a favor. Who knows if I would've even finished massage therapy school and I probably wouldn't have opened my own business if I'd stayed with Earl."

Indignation rolled off Olivia. "What a load of rot, telling you he was sleeping around because you were too busy with classes and work."

Tammy shrugged and turned on the blender, grinding the fruit and ice to a smoothie. "He was an affair waiting to happen. If it'd been up to Earl, I'd still be doing acrylics in his sister's salon and asking him for grocery money each week."

Olivia would never know the half of it. Earl had made Tammy's life hell. A shiver slid down her spine. Just talking about it made her appreciate what a close call she'd had.

Olivia swore again.

"You like that word don't you?"

"It's appropriate."

"Well, at least half of it's on target, but I don't think it's fair to drag his mother into it. Anyway, I'm kicking butt in the best way possible. Living well is the best revenge. I've got my own house, my own business, and I've done it on my own. All of them thought I was nothing without them. Hell, for the longest time, *I* thought I was nothing without them."

Another mood shift struck again and Olivia teared up. "I am so proud of you. You've done great."

"Thanks." Olivia's approval meant a lot to her. "I *have* done great." Tammy loved her small house, her business and her newfound independence. She was doing better than great—not too shabby for the white-trash girl with the bad reputation whose mother abandoned their family and whose father couldn't kick the bottle. And it had only taken her fifteen years and three bad marriages to find herself. She wasn't about to get off track again.

She poured their liquid lunch into two glasses.

"I'd like to propose a toast," Olivia said, hoisting her glass. "Goodbye, Earl."

"I'll drink to that." She clinked her glass against her sister's, elated to close that chapter of her life. She didn't even want to talk about it anymore. She was her own woman now. "And here's to spending the rest of my day off working on my Vitamin D therapy." Tammy laughed at Olivia's blank expression. "I'm going to work on my all-over tan."

"You're nuts. It's November."

"It's gorgeous outside—a record high today and then it's supposed to be twenty-five degrees cooler tomorrow. Plus the Walters' place next door has been sold. That means my naked tanning days are numbered."

And it was one of her favorite things to do. Between a screen of trees and her fence, she couldn't see Mrs. Flander's house to her right at all. Unfortunately, the Walters' backyard offered an unencumbered view of her patio about halfway down the fence line.

"Go for it." Olivia glanced at her watch and jumped up. "Gotta run. We've got a seniors' book club meeting at the library in half an hour. Thanks for the smoothie, congrats on getting rid of Earl and enjoy your afternoon naked."

"Thanks. Maybe I'll get lucky and run into Mr. Right Now." Olivia shook her head. Tammy laughed and pressed several smoothie additive packets into Olivia's hand. "Don't forget to drink one a day. It's good for you and the babelet."

"Yes, boss."

Tammy waited until Olivia reached her car before she closed the front door.

It was time to get naked.

1

"I LIKE IT ALREADY." Niall Fortson stood next to the U-Haul beneath the sprawling oak that encompassed the postage-stamp front yard. He breathed in deeply, filling his lungs with fresh, clean air.

As an army brat, he'd traipsed from military post to military post, all the while craving a place where he could put down roots and start a family. A place similar to his grandparents' small town, where he'd spent his summers chasing fireflies at dusk and fishing the deep pools along the banks of the muddy Cohutta.

Colthersville, Georgia, was just where he wanted to be.

Gigi, a Pomeranian Chihuahua mix, and Memphis, a cream puff disguised as a bull mastiff, clambered out of the moving van.

Cissy Simpson, the local Realtor, kept a careful eye on Gigi and Memphis as she beamed and gestured toward the residential street with its modest frame houses. "It's an older neighborhood, but quiet and the backyards are nice and big." She flashed a professional smile and herded him up the walkway. "Just what you ordered and quite a deal."

He followed Cissy toward the broad steps fronting

the porch. Gigi and Memphis dashed around the yard, marking bushes with the frenzy of dogs in a new place.

"The dogs like it."

"Good." She smiled tightly at the dogs. Definitely a cat person. "Now let's see...the front steps have been replaced. The whole house has a fresh coat of paint...."

His mind wandered while she ran through her litany of the owner's improvements. The rambling frame house with its mullioned windows was a far cry from the brick-fronted Georgian tract mansion he'd shared with Mia in their cookie-cutter subdivision. He already preferred this.

And he'd feel the same even if he wasn't still mildly—okay, actively—pissed off that Mia had flushed eight years together down the toilet rather than marry him. It wasn't Colthersville or the move she'd objected to. They'd always planned on Niall buying into a small-town practice and on getting married. But when the time came, Mia had been willing to make the move but not willing to marry him, regardless of how important it was to him.

She'd dictated they could move on her terms or he could leave alone.

He'd left. The house. The furniture. Her. He'd grabbed his animals, his books, his veterinary journals and a hodgepodge of stuff from his college days that Mia had relegated to the basement, and left. Yeah, it still rankled.

"So, are you ready to see the inside?" Cissy stared at him expectantly.

He shook off the past. "Let me get the cats out first," he said.

Cissy waited by the front door while he retrieved the cat carriers from the front seat of the moving van.

Niall mounted the steps with Tex and Lolita. "This is the new place, guys." The cats blinked, still mellowed by tranquilizers.

"You're a veritable Dr. Doolittle." Cissy eyed the cats much more warmly than the dogs.

"Comes with being a veterinarian. We tend to like animals."

"I see." She obviously didn't get his attempted humor. She opened the front door and gestured him inside. "Welcome home, Dr. Fortson."

Niall stepped inside and settled the cat carriers next to the wall. Time worn hardwood floors smelled of wax. Sunlight slanted through uncurtained windows in the two rooms flanking the shotgun hall, casting diamond patterns on the wood floor. Even without curtains and furniture, it felt welcoming and comfortable.

"The bedrooms are upstairs." Cissy gestured to a craftsman-styled staircase angled to the left.

He'd given her three criteria, a large, fenced yard, a dishwasher and a moderate price tag. Buying Dr. Schill's vet practice had soaked up his cash.

The house's price tag had been moderate. Cissy'd assured him it came with a dishwasher. He whistled for the dogs. "I'd like to check out the backyard."

Cissy carefully avoided the dogs as they charged past, Gigi's toenails clicking a rhythm on the wood floors while Memphis moved through like a small herd of elephants. "It's straight ahead and out through the kitchen. Now, about the kitchen, it's very—" Cissy hesitated, as if searching for a word.

Niall followed her into the room, then stopped in his tracks.

"Turquoise," he supplied.

"Retro," she countered.

"Yeah." Christ. The kitchen hadn't been part of Cissy's cyber home tour. Now he knew why. "I didn't know they made those in turquoise."

Bright lemon yellow walls provided a backdrop for the blue-green appliances. He and Mia had dropped a couple of thousand dollars on a custom-designed refrigerator and dishwasher to match the cabinetry in their kitchen. "It's, uh..."

"Cheery," Cissy suggested with a bright smile. "I hate to run but I've got a two o'clock appointment." She grabbed his hand and pumped it. Ye gods, the woman had the grip of a sumo wrestler. "Welcome to Colthersville and enjoy your new home." She backed toward the hallway. "I'll see myself out. Let me know if I can help you with anything else," she called over her shoulder.

The front door closed behind Cissy and Niall crossed the *cheery* kitchen. He opened the back door and the dogs raced outside, clambering across a wooden deck to the fenced yard beyond.

Niall stepped out on the deck, satisfied. This more than made up for the kitchen. The majority of his half-acre lot sat behind the house, enclosed by a wooden privacy fence. Gigi and Memphis took off across the weed-studded lawn, a canine odd couple. A faint breeze stirred a swing into motion beneath a bare-branched oak. Spent wildflowers choked the lot's back corner. A nostalgic air enveloped the property, as if time had stood still. The kitchen was definitely stuck in the seventies. He grinned at the notion.

The dogs loved it here already. The unmowed grass, although overgrown, appeared healthy. A sense of belonging he'd yearned for all his life enveloped him.

He looked at the property to the right. Whoa. A shapely pair of ankles and feet hung over the end of a chaise lounge. Interest strummed through him. Shrubs hid the rest of the woman—those feet and ankles could only belong to a woman. He'd obviously spent too much time behind the wheel of the moving van if he felt this much interest in a pair of legs—make that one-fifth of a pair of legs.

"Hello," he called, loud enough to carry across the distance. The feet didn't even twitch. "Hi, there." He tried again, louder yet. Still no response. Maybe she was asleep. Or hard of hearing. The feet and ankles were nice, but, hell, she might be older than his own mother, for all he knew.

If he walked over to the fence and down a bit, he could probably see past the shrub. Niall nixed the idea, deliberately turning away. That'd be great. He could move into town and earn a reputation as a Peeping Tom, all in one afternoon. News traveled fast in small towns. *Have you heard? The new vet's a perve.* He laughed into the warm day at the idea.

His laughter died a quick death as Gigi squeezed beneath the fencing—she'd found a hole—and disappeared to the other side. The side belonging to the geriatric sunbather. Damn it to hell. Gigi loved to nibble on toes—one of her more endearing traits.

"Gigi. Come. Come, Gigi," he commanded.

Gigi behaved as usual. She ignored him, launching herself across the neighboring yard like a seven-pound rocket. Niall loped across his yard. Gigi was over there. He was over here. He aimed for damage control.

Just as he reached the fence line, Gigi attacked the bare toes hanging over the chaise. The woman screamed and leaped to her feet.

In an instant, Niall's world tilted on its axis. She wasn't geriatric and she was heart-stopping, blood-pumping naked. Except for a navel ring, earphones and a pair of sunglasses—and they didn't particularly count.

Niall struggled to focus on the woman's face. It was damn hard. She plucked off her earphones.

"Let me guess, you're my new neighbor and *this* belongs to you." She nodded toward Gigi who had commandeered the chaise lounge. Her distinctly southern drawl held more than a note of amusement.

With unhurried movements, the woman tugged the towel from beneath the dog and wrapped it around her, sarong-style, tucking the knot in the cleft of her breasts.

She lowered her glasses and peered over them, her sparkling blue eyes encouraging him to speak up. She appeared more amused than embarrassed. Although totally nude moments ago, she was calm, cool and collected. He, fully clothed, couldn't seem to bumble through an introduction.

"Uh, yeah. Sorry about this. We're your new neighbors. Meet Gigi. She's more bravado than brains. I'm sorry we...uh...interrupted you."

"No problem—I didn't want to burn anyway." Her friendly smile was faintly provocative.

"No. Burning would be bad." Speechlessness was actually preferable to his inane banter.

"Give me a minute and I'll meet you at my gate so you can get Gigi." The woman turned toward her house, displaying an equally impressive towel-covered backside. Some men liked skinny, stick-women. He wasn't one of them. And she was no stick. She glanced over her shoulder "Does she bite?"

"Huh?"

"The dog. Does she bite?" Laughter flavored her southern accent.

"Only unsuspecting toes." He recovered his wit.

Smiling, she turned and disappeared into the house.

Niall felt sure the woman would be wearing more than her towel and navel ring when she showed up at the back gate. He wasn't so sure whether he'd be relieved or disappointed.

But he *did* know he liked the neighborhood already.

BUTT-ASS NAKED *was a helluva way to meet the new neighbor.* There were probably worse ways to meet the new folks other than in her birthday suit, although none immediately came to mind.

Given his slack-jawed response, she'd definitely made an impression. For the first time in as long as she could recall, she'd actually felt self-conscious about her nudity. Apparently he was a new species of man. The ones she knew were the ogling variety. The way he'd carefully looked her in the eye rather than ogle her had compelled her to cover herself. But a hint of her bad girl tendencies had remained because she'd found the situation *stimulating.*

He was fully dressed—well, as far as she could tell, with only his head and shoulders sticking up over her fence—and still she'd felt a powerful tug of attraction. As she'd told Olivia earlier, she was in a bad way.

Out of deference to her new neighbor's sensibilities, and the wife and two kids probably lurking in the background, Tammy pulled on her jeans and shirt, which she'd draped over the kitchen chair, the fabric playing against her still stimulated parts.

She wasn't kowtowing to public opinion, but she'd become a little more circumspect since she'd gone into business for herself. She glanced down at her plunging neckline and hip huggers and laughed. It *was* more conservative than wearing a towel.

She stepped out onto the patio. There, Gigi lounged indolently on the chaise, full of bold attitude. Tammy laughed at the audacity of the funny-looking little dog. "Come on, you. Your family wants you back." She walked past the dog and snapped her fingers.

Surprisingly, Gigi hopped down and flounced along beside her.

The lush grass cushioned her bare feet as she crossed the yard to her waiting neighbor. The man's dark brown hair, a few weeks past a good haircut, glinted in the sun. Nice square jaw, his hooked nose a shade too big by most standards but very masculine. Even now, fully clothed, self-consciousness caused her to flush as she approached him.

"One small dog returned to you." She opened the gate and the little dog pranced through.

A worn T-shirt hung on him, revealing well-muscled arms. Even though he was built like a former linebacker—who'd managed not to go to fat—his stance lacked the aggressive arrogance so common in big men. Nerves fluttered low in her belly.

"On the porch, Gigi," he ordered with affectionate tolerance, then turned to face Tammy. Her breath hitched in her throat. Oh, baby! Up close, he possessed the most extraordinary, soulful, brown eyes— yummy, sinfully rich pools of dark chocolate flecked with caramel framed by long dark lashes. They were a sensuous contrast to the masculine lines of his face and his strong nose. Their impact coursed through her all the way to her toes and sent her mind tumbling between the sheets.

"I apologize again for Gigi's bad manners. I'm Niall Fortson." He extended a massive hand.

Hadn't she heard once that the size of a man's hand, or was it his feet—instinctively she glanced down—indicated the size of... She yanked her gaze up and her mind out of the gutter. She had to stop thinking this way.

"I'm Tammy Bran-uh, Cooper," she stumbled over the last name, but now was as good a time as any to go back to her maiden name. "No harm done with Gigi." She grasped his hand. His palm was warm and dry, his clasp sure and solid, and his touch echoed through her, setting off sparks. She desperately needed a good...dose of control. One touch and she was ready to jump him.

Her hand still tingled, even after the handshake ended. Actually his touch had more than her hand tingling. She checked out his ring finger. Naked. Of course, the lack of a wedding ring didn't mean much. Any minute now she expected a perky blonde to bounce around the corner with a couple of cute-as-pie kids in tow. Gigi had *woman's dog* written all over her. Tammy discreetly squinted past him to his front porch.

"Are you looking for something?" He glanced over his shoulder.

So much for discretion. "Just thought I'd meet the rest of the family."

Niall whistled. A massive dog lumbered out the front door. "Tammy meet Memphis. Memphis, Tammy Cooper."

Memphis hiked a leg before ambling over to sniff her crotch in greeting—definitely a man's dog. "Uh, hi there," she offered. Good grief, her entire hand would fit in the dog's massive mouth.

"He's harmless," Niall reassured her.

"I'll take your word for it." She wasn't nearly as comfortable with this beast as she was with the toe-biter.

He laughed, a low pleasing rumble that slid over her like a warm blanket on a cold night. "So, you've met Memphis and Gigi. The cats are still in their carriers. They don't travel well so I sedated them before we left." He grimaced.

Okay, this was why she usually skipped subtlety. It didn't get her anywhere. She'd met her fair share of married men who conveniently forgot to mention the wife and kids. She'd openly fish and if he didn't bite she'd point blank ask him if he was married. "*We* as in the rest of your family?"

He grinned and she realized he'd known all along she wanted to find out he was married. "*We* as in me and the animals. No kids. And my ex-live-in—or significant other, whatever you want to call her—stayed with the house in Oklahoma City."

The significant other business surprised her. Niall

Fortson didn't look like the shacking up type. She didn't exactly know what the shacking up type looked like but it wasn't him. The ex-significant other explained Gigi.

"Gigi belonged to your ex?" She'd bet the farm.

Surprise flitted across his face. "How'd you know?"

Aha. Her instincts hadn't failed her. "Lucky guess. How'd you wind up with her? The dog, not your ex." Shoot her for being nosy, but inquiring minds wanted to know.

"Mia wanted Gigi and then decided she was too high-maintenance."

Mia. She sounded like an urbane sitcom character. Tammy had a feeling the woman had been far more high-maintenance than the dog.

He peered over her shoulder in teasing imitation. "What about your family?"

Tammy laughed at his easy ribbing. "It's just me." It felt good to say that—no, make that great. "My ex-husbands, all three of them, stayed with the houses." Might as well air the multiple divorces up front.

"Probably a good thing. It could get crowded with three ex-husbands hanging around." Niall quirked his mouth in a lopsided smile that started in his eyes and radiated to engage the rest of his face. A small scar along his upper lip added a hint of rugged sexiness. Tammy's pulse quickened and a slow heat curled through her. *A sense of humor and a bone-melting smile.* "Any pets?"

"No. No pets."

"And now you're living next to *Wild Kingdom*." Another dose of that smile and her heart rate did another bump and grind. "I'll try to keep Gigi on my side of the fence."

"Your animals are fine. I don't have anything against animals—I just don't want the responsibility." Or another gaping wound that came with losing a pet. Once had been enough. Pets and kids were cool as long as they belonged to someone else.

Thank God she'd had the sense to go on the pill at a young age and not jump into motherhood during any of her marriages. She'd been thrown into the mother role when Martha Rae, as she'd thought of her mom for years now, abandoned their family. Not only had Tammy done a lousy job mothering Olivia and their brother Marty, she'd had enough of it to last a lifetime.

"They do require commitment." Did she simply imagine it or did his ready smile falter a bit? He obviously had a thing for animals.

"What brings you to Colthersville?" Tammy asked, filling in what had become an awkward silence. And she was curious.

"I'm a vet. I'm joining Dr. Schill's practice."

Didn't that just rip? Yeah, he had a thing for animals. "Congratulations. Dr. Schill's a good vet, even if he is an old goat."

Surprise raised his brows. "Okay. Thanks for the information."

She thought she'd shown some restraint. She positively loathed the man. She could've called him a lech.

It was a much more accurate description. "Sorry. I call 'em the way I see 'em. I was married to Dr. Schill's son."

Niall winced. "Things didn't end well?"

The beginning had been great with Allen and the ending had been fine. It was the in between that had stunk on ice. From the day they'd married, Dr. Schill acted as if Tammy wasn't good enough for his son. Then the randy old goat had cornered her in the kitchen and put the move on her one Thanksgiving. A well-placed knee had taken care of the immediate situation. Later, when she'd mentioned it to Allen, he'd defended his father, claiming Tammy had misunderstood his dad. In her book, it was difficult to misunderstand the old guy squeezing her breasts. Her marriage had gone downhill from there.

She shrugged. "It was a long time ago. Allen was my second husband. He's remarried and he and Jenna have two kids now, so all's well."

An ant marched across her bare foot. She shifted to one foot and nudged it off with her toe, swaying slightly. Niall reached out and wrapped his hand around her upper arm. "Steady."

"Thanks." A soft shiver slid down her spine at his touch. He dropped his hand and in an instant she was back to two feet firmly on the ground, but the heat evoked by his touch continued to radiate through her.

"It's safe to mention you're the girl next door?"

She laughed aloud at the idea of her being the girl next door. Like any other place, small or otherwise,

Colthersville had its share of gossips and she'd given them plenty to talk about over the years. It'd take about two seconds for anyone in Colthersville to fill him in on her reputation.

"That'd be a poor choice of words. I don't think anyone who knows me would buy into the girl next door label. I'm the resident bad girl."

And he might just be Mr. Right Now.

2

"BAD IS A RELATIVE TERM. You don't strike me as bad at all." As a rule, Niall liked people—almost as much as he liked animals—but in the span of five minutes he found himself inordinately drawn to Tammy Cooper.

A cynic would've said it was due to his first glimpse of her naked, but it was more than that. Of course, he'd never forget that first sight of her—and she wasn't going to let him, either.

"In case you missed it, I was naked when I met you." *He would've had to be dead to have missed it but, thank you, Jesus, he'd been alive, cognizant and fully appreciative.* "Has it been your experience that nice girls sit around naked?" Her amazing blue eyes sparkled. The little vixen was thoroughly enjoying needling him.

"Actually, I have very little experience with women sitting around naked. Nice or otherwise." If she wanted to play the bad girl, he'd play her straight man.

Niall propped his arm against the fence and really looked at Tammy Cooper—a much safer proposition now that she was fully clothed. Bottle-blond hair just this side of brassy—he'd known from when she jumped up earlier she wasn't a true blonde. Sky-blue eyes with a hint of wariness beneath all the makeup. Gauzy, white shirt with a plunging neckline and the provocative thrust of dusky nipples. Bare midriff with a gold navel ring—he had no clue why that was such a turn-on but it was—above low-slung jeans. Bare feet with a toe ring. Very sexy. "However, I hardly think that naked qualifies you as a bad girl."

She tilted her head, her hair sweeping against her shoulder. She smelled like coconut and her golden skin glistened with suntan lotion. "Did you miss the three husbands I mentioned?" A thread of tension ran through her laughing banter.

No. He hadn't missed her obvious attempt to warn him off. Instead of off-putting, he found it intriguing. "Duly noted." Niall, known for his congeniality, discovered a perverse pleasure in arguing with her. "I thought you were very nice about Gigi. You didn't throw a screaming fit when she surprised you." Mia damn well would've and Cissy, the Realtor, had certainly maintained her distance. "Instead you laughed."

His comment coaxed another laugh and a one-shouldered shrug, which did incredible things to the low neckline of her blouse, which in turn did incredible things to his breathing. She had a nice laugh—warm, throaty, sexy. Hell, she turned simple breathing into a sexy experience.

"Tiny Mite the Attack Dog was funny." Her husky voice stroked through him, firing all those impulses inside that hadn't fired in a long time—perhaps ever.

He and Mia had shared a healthy sexual relationship but he'd never experienced this kind of reaction to a woman before. And it wasn't just because he'd seen her naked. She exuded an innate sensuality that brought to mind sweat-slicked bodies and hot, sticky sex.

Inside her house, the phone rang. She stepped away.

"I'll try and keep Gigi in my yard."

"Don't worry about it." She winked at him. Deliberately. Provocatively. "And I'll let you in on a secret. Even bad girls like to laugh."

He didn't think he'd forget it anytime soon.

INVITING NIALL Fortson over for dinner was the neighborly thing to do, she reasoned as she rubbed fresh, pungent garlic and black pepper over two thick steaks. It had nothing to do with his sense of humor, his chocolate brown eyes or the heat tremors he'd set off with a single handshake. Well, maybe it had a little to do with that, but mostly it was a matter of being neighborly. She knew all about moving into a neighborhood without a friendly welcome. It was the pits.

The man traveled light, she'd give him that. It was a small moving van and it hadn't taken him long to unload. He'd carried in a Nautilus machine with apparent ease when she'd returned from the grocery store earlier, which explained his nicely muscled shoulders and arms.

She washed and dried her hands. She was being

weird and neurotic to be so nervous about inviting him into her space. For sweet pity's sake, it was a house, not some inner sanctum. Before she could change her mind again and weenie out, she slipped out the back door. Tammy crossed the yard to his front door and rang the bell.

Sharp, staccato barking erupted on the opposite side of the door. "It's me. From next door."

Surprisingly, the barking stopped. Within seconds Niall opened the door, a towel in one hand. "Hi." A welcoming smile lit his eyes and set off an internal heat wave. "I just got out of the shower," he added with a charming note of self-consciousness.

That visual image left her nearly breathless. She didn't have to close her eyes to imagine hot water sluicing over his bare, male, hair-roughened body. Droplets of water clinging to his broad chest, the flat planes of his belly, the jutting line of his...

She'd been good way too long. She'd focused on her business and her house. Now she was in close proximity to a decent man and she felt like a nymphomaniac turned loose on a football team. Overwrought, oversexed and out of control.

She tried to focus. Where were they? Oh, yeah. Him. Just out of the shower.

"I see." Damp footprints glistened against the dark hardwood floor. Niall's wet hair stuck up as if he'd just toweled it. He'd traded in jeans and a T-shirt for a pair of sweats and a T-shirt. There was a disquieting intimacy and eroticism in his bare feet, with their masculine sprinkling of hair. There was also something inherently sexy in his tousled hair, the scent of male deodorant and warm, damp skin. "Is this a bad time?" she managed to ask.

"No. Not at all." Gigi danced around Tammy's legs. "Back off, Gigi," he ordered with a shake of his head. He glanced at Tammy, his brown eyes full of laughing apology. "She likes you. Unfortunately, Gigi is obnoxious around anyone who is the object of her affections."

"She's fine." Tammy found the little dog's outgoing cuteness disconcerting—she didn't ever want to feel attachment to an animal again—but not obnoxious.

Niall stood aside. "Come in if you're not afraid of the boxes and the beasts."

Tammy stepped into his house, past his male, fresh-showered scent. "I came over to offer dinner. Nothing fancy. Just steak, salad and potato."

"How fast can I say yes?"

For an instant she thought he might scoop her up and kiss her, he looked so excited at the prospect of food. And there were worse things that could happen. He had a nice firm mouth and that intriguing scar on his upper lip.

She'd been pretty sure Niall wouldn't turn down her invitation to a hot meal. Exactly what kind of invitation would he turn down, if any?

"That was fast enough. Why don't you come over in about half an hour? We can wash down some chips and salsa with cold beers before dinner."

"Cold beer?" Niall looked like he'd died and gone to heaven.

"Yep." And if he looked any sexier, with his tousled hair and hint of a five o'clock shadow darkening his jaw, she couldn't be held accountable for her actions.

"Hot salsa?" His voice held a ragged edge.

She swallowed hard, her breath as ragged as his tone. The connection between food and sex had never been so achingly apparent. "It's the only way I like it. The hotter, the better."

"I'll be over as soon as I change and clean up a bit. I need to find my razor." He ran a hand along his jaw and offered a rueful smile.

"You're fine." Unshaven *and* undressed would be even finer.

"It'll get better once I unpack."

She'd been so caught up in Niall she hadn't paid any attention to the house. Now she openly looked around. To the left of the door, the Nautilus machine sat in the middle of the dining room beneath a wrought-iron chandelier. In the den, to her right, a worn bookcase stood sentinel to an equally worn sofa, a scarred coffee table, a floor lamp that reminded her of the one at Pops's house, and half a dozen moving boxes. He owned some butt-ugly furniture, that was for sure.

"You travel pretty light."

Niall shrugged and his expression tightened. He jerked a thumb toward the den. "This was stuff from my days in vet school."

Hmmm. She'd bet a dollar to a donut the ex in Oklahoma was parked on a much better-looking sofa.

"I'd offer you a tour, but I'm sure you've seen the house before."

"Actually, I've never been inside. An older couple lived here before. They moved out a few months after I moved in. I've lived next door for less than a year." She didn't mention it had taken almost the whole seven months she'd lived in the house for the neighbors to accept her. Tammy wasn't sure whether they'd been disappointed or relieved when time had proven she was just another home owner, not a wild orgy hostess. The fact of the matter was, Tammy was a bit of a loner. Olivia was her only visitor, except for the time her brother Marty had stopped in to borrow twenty bucks to buy a bottle of booze.

"Then how about the grand tour?" Without waiting for an answer, he started. "To your left is the former dining room, now known as the workout room." She chuckled at his very guylike grin. "To your right is the den. The one-eared tabby on the back of the sofa is Tex. The orange cat peering between the boxes is Lolita." When she heard her name, the marmalade cat limped from her hiding spot and leaped to the sofa to join Tex—pretty agile for a cat with only three legs.

"Hi, Tex. Hi, Lolita." Tex returned her greeting with a basilisk stare and Lolita yawned daintily. They were the most pathetic-looking cats she'd ever seen. Niall Fortson seemed to have a soft spot for rejects.

"They stay indoors, so they won't rush your yard

the way Gigi did," he explained with a smile as he ushered her down the hall to a doorway at the end. His fingers rested lightly against the small of her back and awareness whispered along her nerve endings. "Prepare yourself." He looked at her with a hint of consternation. "Too bad you don't have any shades with you." He threw open the door. "Behold the kitchen."

Beautiful sunny walls embraced turquoise countertops and appliances. It reminded her of a Mexican plaza on a warm afternoon. "Awesome. I love it."

"You do?" His expression verged on comical. Obviously that wasn't his take.

"Of course. How could anyone ever be depressed in such a great room?" She couldn't frown in this room even if she wanted to. "Doesn't it make you want to smile when you walk in?"

"Uh..." Apparently not.

Tammy pressed on, caught up in the room's potential. "Some orange—well, really more like tangerine—curtains with the yellow and turquoise in them would tie everything together. Maybe toss in a splash of lime green. Funky but fun, in a happy kind of way."

If that didn't scare the bejezus out of him, nothing would. Men freaked when women made suggestions about their space, place or person. Jerry had nearly lost his mind when she'd vetoed hanging a mounted deer head in their bedroom—like she wanted a dead Bambi eyeballing her when she was trying to sleep or do other things. Niall looked a tad bemused, much like when he'd seen her naked earlier. "Orange?"

"Hmm. Tangerine. Trust me. I've been into this decorating thing lately." She'd had a blast with her own house, discovering a sense of style she never knew she possessed.

"Okay. I can use all the help I can get." He looked around the room, as if he could actually see it taking on a new appeal. "Funky but fun."

Tammy leaned against the counter and laughed. "You've never done funky before?"

Niall ran a hand over his hair which did nothing to smooth it down. "No. But I wouldn't mind giving it a try. I wanted a fresh start." He glanced at the turquoise refrigerator and shook his head. "It's definitely funky compared to matching cherry cabinetry."

"It sounds hideously traditional and conservative." Tammy would take the wild, bold beauty of this room over matching cherry any day.

Niall laughed. "I wouldn't call it hideous, but it was conservative, except for the price tag. I'll try to remember tangerine with yellow and turquoise."

"Just go into Bergman's and look a little lost. Women will fall all over themselves to help you."

"I can certainly manage to look lost. That won't be a problem. I'm not sure about the falling all over themselves business." On some men, the modesty would've been calculated. Niall actually seemed clueless that the single women of Colthersville would be on him like white on rice.

"Trust me on this. *I'm* sure and I'm a woman."

"I noticed." The husky note in his voice and the look in his eyes trailed heat through her.

Awareness arced between them. She eased her tongue along her dry bottom lip and he clenched his jaw. A whine and a scratch at the back door eased the tension of a man and a woman in close quarters and brought them back to two neighbors chatting in the kitchen. Niall opened the door.

"I know where the clinic is, but other than that I'm clueless. What and where is Bergman's?" he asked as the Big Dog lumbered in and ambled over to sniff Tammy.

Time for her to go. She didn't trust Big Dog with his crotch-sniffing and enormous jaws. No one could ever accuse Niall of being a shallow pet owner—he hadn't chosen his animals based on beauty, that was for sure.

She headed back down the hall toward the front door. "It's the local everything store. Just watch out for Henrietta Williams, the owner. She's a woman with a mission—finding a husband for her daughter Candy."

Niall followed, his masculine scent of soap and de-odorant teasing her from behind. "And what would be so bad about that?"

He had to ask? "You could wake up and find your-self married before you knew what hit you."

He reached around her, close enough that she felt his body heat, and opened the door for her. "I'm ready to settle down."

Tammy stepped out onto the porch, away from temptation. He was sexy, single...and looking to get married?

What a shame.

3

NIALL TOOK the long way to Tammy's via the sidewalk rather than across the yard. Despite the warmth of the day, the temperature had plummeted when the sun disappeared. Between the crisp air and the colorful Christmas decorations on the houses, it felt and looked like late November.

Multicolored lights blinked on a Christmas tree in Tammy's front window. A plastic nativity set glowed on her front lawn. He wasn't sure whether he was the luckiest or the unluckiest sod in the world to be living next door to Tammy Cooper. She was sexy, flirty and simply being around her threw him seriously off balance. Niall didn't do off-kilter. He expected things to be a certain way and they usually were.

His stomach rumbled as he knocked on the front door. He was starving. A fast-food lunch snagged from a drive-thru along the way had been a long time ago. He'd accept a meal from Genghis Khan.

Tammy opened the door with a smile that did dangerous things to his pulse.

"Hi, come on in."

She looked and smelled a whole lot better than Genghis. She'd changed into a black shirt and pants that hugged her feminine curves. Bracelets encircled half the length between her wrist and forearm. Her scent, an exotic blend of spices, tantalized him. A harem girl fantasy popped into his tired, overwrought brain and refused to budge. Her wearing only those bracelets and a bunch of veils. Smooth gold skin. Navel ring. Her exotic fragrance.

Niall stepped inside and her arm brushed against his. Heat sizzled though him at the brief contact. What kind of heat would an intentional caress generate? Maybe he was simply tired and hungry but she blew his composure to hell. He turned to face her as she closed the door behind him. "I brought a six-pack of beer. Unfortunately, it's warm, but I didn't want to show up empty-handed."

She took the package. "You didn't have to do that, but thanks."

Niall looked around the room, convinced that was a better plan than gawking at her.

If his kitchen was happy, her house was nearly ecstatic. From outside, it looked like the other neighborhood houses, but inside it was bright and bold. Yellow-gold walls and furniture in a mix of reds, purples and bright blues created a room that was comfortable and inviting without being fussy. "This is great."

For a moment he glimpsed something akin to insecurity in her eyes—as if she'd been nervous about his response to her house. Quick as a flash it was gone and she smiled, obviously pleased by his response. "Yeah. I like it. Sort of vintage meets eclectic. I'm still working on it, but it's been fun. That's one of the great things about living alone. You only have to please yourself." She arched her brow. "I bet Mia never let you keep your workout equipment in the dining room."

Niall grinned at the thought of his Nautilus machine sandwiched between Ethan Allen dining room pieces. "How'd you know?"

"Woman's intuition." Her slow smile spiraled heat through him. "Come on. If you don't mind hanging out in the kitchen. You can put a dent in the chips and salsa while I make the salad. You must be ravenous."

"I wouldn't turn food down. Thanks for inviting me over. Something smells good." His stomach growled as backup.

"Bread and baked potatoes. The steaks will only take a minute." He followed her, mesmerized by the sway of her hips and the curve of her back. She pointed to a small hallway to the right. "Bathroom and two bedrooms over there. This is really more of a cottage than a house but it's mine." The note of pride in her declaration was unmistakable. "And here's the kitchen."

At least a dozen flickering candles, of various shapes and sizes, casts shadows on the walls, creating a cozy intimacy in the galley kitchen despite the regular lighting over the sink. From the wax puddles, Niall surmised Tammy was into a candlelit kitchen, guest or no guest. Vintage Al Green crooned from a cabinet-mounted CD player. Lots of atmosphere. Very sexy. Very relaxing. "Very nice."

"Thanks. Have a seat and I'll get you something to drink. How about one of those beers you drooled over earlier?"

"I'm holding you to it." Niall settled on a stool at a tile-topped island that doubled as a table in the compact kitchen. A large bowl of chips, salsa and guacamole sat in the middle of the island.

"One beer coming up." She opened the fridge and bent forward, molding her black slacks across her heart-shaped bottom and damn near giving him a heart attack. "Help yourself to the chips and salsa. Be careful with the salsa. It's hot."

"That's what you said earlier. I'm sure I can handle it." He stared at the smooth expanse of skin bared by her shirt riding up above the waist of her pants, not nearly as confident he could handle himself around her.

She straightened, two beer bottles in hand and a smile lighting face. "Ah, a man after my own heart."

She pulled a couple of frosty mugs from the freezer and opened the bottles. "How do you like it? Head or no head?"

Holy mother of Christ. His earlier harem girl fantasy supplied a mental image that left him happy to be seated. It promised to be one long night if he continued to read sexual meaning into her every utterance. "Head, please."

She offered another slow, sexy smile that sizzled through him. "Coming right up."

Yeah, he was.

"I like head, as well. There you are." She carefully placed the beer on the tile in front of him.

"Thanks."

She sat across from him. Her foot skimmed his calf, sending heat spiraling through him. "Sorry," she murmured as she shifted.

The moment pulsed with a sensuality that left him breathless. Her scent. The candles. The music. Her touch. Her provocative comments.

"Please. Have some."

He gave way to temptation and sampled what was in front of him. "Good chips and salsa." Hot enough to keep him awake but not incendiary. He took a long pull of beer, relishing the cold bite of hops and foam against his tongue and throat. "Ahh, just the thing at the end of a move."

"Why Colthersville?" she asked. Niall noticed her upper lip was slightly larger than her lower lip, giving her mouth a sensuous pout.

"I grew up a Navy brat. Sixteen different schools from kindergarten to high school. Of all the places we lived, I liked the south the best—the people, the weather, the food. Plus I spent my summers in a small town, Raeburn, with my grandparents. I knew from the time I was a kid, small-town life was for me. When I heard Dr. Schill was selling his practice, I went for it.

Colthersville seems like a nice place to settle down and raise a family."

Slightly embarrassed, Niall realized he'd just offered a long-winded soliloquy of his life. And that was probably more information than she wanted or needed. She was too easy to talk to. "What about you? You said you'd only lived here a couple of months?"

Tammy sipped her beer. White flecks of foam clung to her upper lip. She swiped her tongue along the full line of her mouth, devastating his concentration and composure. "My roots run deep in Colthersville. I was born and raised here. I only bought this house eight months ago. I'd been living with Pops after Earl and I split up."

She spoke matter of factly about her divorce. Not that he wanted her crying in her beer, but she didn't seem particularly brokenhearted or pissed or bitter— all very real emotions he'd seen in other divorced couples. He wasn't brokenhearted and he wasn't bitter, but he was pissed about his breakup with Mia. Maybe she'd worked through all of the above. "How long have you been divorced?"

She circled the rim of her mug with her fingertip. "Almost twenty-four hours." She laughed at the surprise that must've shown on his face. "How about you? Well, not divorced but, ya know, splitsville?"

"Things were over a couple of months ago. I wanted to get married. She didn't. I stayed in the house until it was time for me to move."

She crumbled a chip into small pieces on her saucer. "That must've been a party."

It had been damn awkward. "Luckily it was a big house and we tried to stay out of each other's way."

"Do you miss her?" Her soft question surprised him. No one had asked him that.

Denial sat on the tip of his tongue, driven by pride. But the sincere curiosity on Tammy's face prompted him to say what he hadn't faced before now. "Yeah, I guess I do. We were friends. At least we were 'til the end."

"Maybe you'll get back together." She pushed her chin-length hair behind her ear.

"No." That wasn't pride talking, just surety. "There's not a lot of middle ground when one person wants to get married and the other one doesn't. Even that aside, it felt final when I left. It's over." For the first time he could say it without a bitter note.

She nodded, her blue eyes inscrutable. "Earl and I tried a year's separation, but it was over when I moved out."

"Do you miss him?"

"I did at first. Until I realized how much I liked being on my own."

He was ridiculously relieved she wasn't pining for her ex-husband.

"The papers came today," she continued. "Sunbathing is my way of celebrating!"

It was a provocative reminder. "Do you do that often?" he asked, recalling with gut-clenching clarity her full, dusky-tipped breasts, the glint of her navel ring against her golden skin, the tangle of curls nestled between her thighs and the length of her legs.

"Which one? Divorce or sunbathe naked?" Her smile seduced. "Neither one anymore. That was my third strike and I'm out of the marriage game for good—" he didn't have to be a boy genius to figure *that* one out "—and as for the other, I don't want to upset the new neighbors."

"I can't speak for the other neighbors, but don't let me cramp your style." He wasn't normally much of a flirt, but Tammy's easy sensuality inspired him.

"Ah, but can I trust Gigi to leave my naked toes alone? They're very sensitive, you know." She glanced at him from beneath her lashes. One playful comment, a provocative look and she totally turned him on.

"I'm sure they are." The thought of sensitive naked toes and sensitive naked other parts left him aching. Talking about something other than naked parts might not be a bad idea. Besides, he found that the more he knew about her, the more he wanted to know. "What do you do?"

"I'm a massage therapist." *Oh, hell, that just intensified the naked parts fantasies lurking at the back of his mind.* "I started my own business five months ago and it's going well." Her husky laugh held an underlying note of self-consciousness. "I finally figured out what I wanted to be when I grew up. Before that I did a little bit of everything. I was a nail technician, a waitress, and a grocery store checkout clerk." She propped her chin in her hand and fixed him with her bright blue eyes. "How about you? How long have you been a vet?"

She looked as if she really cared and wasn't just making polite conversation. Actually, Tammy impressed him as doing exactly what she wanted and the niceties be damned. She'd certainly been forthright about Schill, her ex-husbands and her reputation.

"I finished vet school five years ago, but I knew that's what I wanted to do from the time I was a kid. Except for the summer I was six and wanted to drive an ice-cream truck."

Tammy laughed, "Talk about a shift in ambition. Why a vet?"

"It just felt right. I've always liked animals and I like to fix things. I drove my mom nuts bringing home sick animals."

Throughout the meal preparation and dinner, they discussed everything from movies—she preferred suspense rather than his action thrillers—to the NFL playoffs. With a start, Niall realized they'd finished eating some time ago and a number of the candles had burned low.

Reluctantly, he pushed away from the island. "Thanks for a great dinner. I should be getting home." He couldn't remember the last time he'd enjoyed himself so much. "Let me help with the dishes before I go."

"They're no big deal." Tammy blew off his offer.

"Good. Then it shouldn't take us long to get them done."

"A man who does dishes—let this get out and the women really will swamp you."

Twice she'd alluded to other women swamping him. Was she trying to tell him she wasn't interested? But he hadn't gotten that impression at all. She felt the attraction between them—he'd seen it in her eyes more than once tonight.

"Didn't any of your husbands ever help out in the kitchen?" He was no saint, but his mother had taught him and his brother and sister to clean up after themselves, and he'd figured out early on that cutting the work in half left more time for him and Mia. Not only was he not into having someone wait on him, it led to sex on a much more regular basis.

"Jerry, my first husband, thought *wife* was another word for *maid*. I was so young and dumb at seventeen, I went along with it, but Allen and Earl were okay."

"Seventeen?" That seemed incredibly young. The summer Niall was seventeen, his father'd been stationed in Southern California at Point Magu. He'd spent his time cruising the Pacific Highway in his buddy's beat-up convertible and learning to surf. Tammy'd already been married.

"It seemed like the thing to do at the time." Her husky voice feathered across his skin. He turned to pass the plates to her as she spoke. Squeezed into the tight space between the island and the sink, her hip bumped his thigh and his arm pressed against hers.

He'd never been aware of a woman to such a devastating degree. He felt on fire for her.

"Do you regret getting married so young?" He didn't normally quiz people this way, but he felt compelled to know more about her—everything about her.

She looked up at him, her eyes serious. "Regret's pointless—a waste of energy. We're shaped by our past. If you regret where you've been, how can you like who you've become?" She closed the dishwasher and dried her hands. As if blown away by a gust of wind, her intensity vanished and she was once again flashing a naughty-girl smile. "Now I'm going to give you directions to the grocery store because the neighbors will talk if you show up for breakfast tomorrow morning."

Tammy pulled a pen and paper out of a drawer. Bracing one hand on the island, Niall leaned over her shoulder. He forgot to read what she was writing, distracted by her nearness. An errant lock of her hair brushed against his chin as she looked up. Her breath fanned against his chin, her scent wrapped around him. In the light of the flickering candles and small lamp, her skin glowed and her blue eyes darkened.

God help him, but it was a subtle form of mental torture that he'd seen her naked before and now she was close and real and he wanted to see her naked again. But more than that, even though he'd spent the whole evening talking and laughing with her, he had the distinct impression several layers concealed the real Tammy Cooper. She'd been blunt and free and easy with personal information, but she'd only let him see what she wanted him to see.

Longing, unlike any he'd known before, gripped him. He reached out to touch her cheek, the yearning to test the satin of her skin against his finger and feel the fullness of her mouth against his almost a physical ache. Her lips were so close, so tempting, he could feel her warm breath against his mouth, could almost taste her...

At the last minute, sanity prevailed and he reached for the paper instead. He'd almost made a total ass of himself by repaying her courtesy and hospitality by making a pass at her.

For a moment something flickered across her face. Disappointment? Vulnerability? Niall's own emotions were so tossed, he wasn't sure. He just knew he needed to get out of here. "Thank you. For everything."

Tammy escorted him to the front door, once again in control, her unguarded moment gone. "You're welcome for everything." She leaned forward, her body maddingly close. Her scent, her heat drew him closer til the tips of her nipples seared him through their layers of clothes. With a soft laugh, Tammy tugged his head down, her fingers soft against his neck. She pressed a quick, hot kiss to his mouth. The kiss was almost over before it'd begun. She opened the door for him. "Good night, Niall. My number's on the paper. Give me a call if you need anything."

At that moment Niall realized the distinct difference between want and need.

TAMMY WELCOMED her regular work routine the next morning. Last night's dinner with Niall had left her restless. For the first time since she'd moved into her house, she'd known the discontent of her own company once he'd gone home. Worse yet, self-pleasure with Big Ben had fallen short of the mark, merely accentuating the longing Niall had stirred in her. Two D-cell batteries couldn't mimic his breath stirring against her neck or the cautious heat in his dark eyes. She'd been so sure he was going to kiss her. She'd practically trembled with anticipation. She'd been so surprised when he hadn't.... He'd left her no option except to kiss him instead and give him something to think about overnight. She'd certainly thought about it. And now she had a business to think about.

Tammy unlocked the old-fashioned, glass-fronted door that faced the town square. Saturdays were always booked and today was no exception. One of the smartest business decisions she'd made was taking Fridays off and opening Saturdays to accommodate clients' work schedules or stay-at-home moms who needed to leave the kidlets with dad to make an appointment.

Her first appointment, Willette Tidwell, was in fifteen minutes, which meant Tammy had half an hour to kill, since Willette would be late to her own funeral when the time came.

She knelt on the Harlequin-tiled floor and leaned in to arrange an orange-ginger scented gift set beneath the Christmas tree in the narrow window front. Just enough time to finish the Christmas display. She'd sold three gift sets already this week.

The bell tinkled as the door opened behind her. She twisted around. Uh-oh. Lowell Evans.

"Hey, Tammy."

"What's up, Lowell?" She rose to her feet, sure she knew why Lowell had stopped by. She'd told him she wouldn't go out with him until her divorce was final. She was a free woman today.

"Heard your divorce came through." *Bingo.* The gleam in his bedroom-blue eyes bordered on predatory.

Why wasn't his frank appraisal and appreciation eliciting even a quiver, especially after her ten and a half month hiatus? Once upon a time, that look had left her hot and bothered. Now it just left her bothered.

Tammy laughed, shaking her head. "I know news travels fast in this town, but it was just yesterday."

"Yeah, well, Earl mentioned it at Cecil's last night."

She'd celebrated by sunbathing naked. Earl had celebrated with a beer or two at Cecil's Bar and Grill. Actually, Earl wouldn't have stopped at two unless he'd changed drastically in the past year. That'd been yet one more irreconcilable difference when they'd split up. Earl had grown increasingly fond of a inebriation. She'd grown up with a drunk—she loved Pops but she'd spent one too many nights as a child and a teenager looking after an alcoholic—by God, she wasn't going to remain married to one. She hadn't considered sobriety and faithfulness unreasonable requests.

She almost asked Lowell just how wasted Earl had been, but left it alone. Frankly, Scarlett, she didn't give a damn.

Instead she looked at Lowell, which wasn't a hardship 'cause Lowell was a bonafide hottie. A tough guy in a tight-jeans-and-tattoo, badass kind of way. Actually, just the kind of guy she'd always been attracted to. Past tense. Lowell wasn't doing a thing for her now.

"You're looking good, babe." He leaned against the door with a swagger and raked her with hungry eyes. "Hot. So, now that you're footloose and fancy-free, how about you and me going out?"

Lowell was the spitting image of Brad Pitt and she'd always had a thing for Brad. Her hormones should've been having a field day at the prospect of going out with him. She'd always maintained a gal had to grab a chance when it presented itself. Now, here was Lowell, opportunity personified, and she wasn't interested.

Not the way she'd been interested when she'd felt Niall's heat in the close confines of her kitchen last night or when she'd kissed him by the front door. *That* memory alone notched up her temperature.

She shook her head. "I don't think so."

Lowell's cocky grin faded. "You don't think so?"

He wasn't nearly so sexy with his mouth hanging open.

"That's right." She turned to straighten the magazines on the table between the two armchairs. Her waiting room was small, but that was okay. There was never more than one person waiting at a time.

"Why the hell don't you want to go out with me?"

Because she'd fricking said so should've been good enough. Lowell's arrogant incredulity was beginning to work her nerves. "Lowell, I don't owe you an explanation. I've said *no* so leave it at that."

Lowell wasn't a happy camper. He wasn't used to being turned down.

"I may not still be interested when you decide you are," he warned, crossing his arms over his chest like a petulant child.

His attitude weakened his case and strengthened her resolve. A grown man sulking was so *not* sexy. "I'll take that chance."

"Baby, I could play you like a violin. You don't know what you're missing."

"I'm pretty sure I do." Lowell struck her as remarkably similar to Earl, Jerry, Allen and all the other men in between. Same book, different page. And suddenly she was ready to read a different book.

Willette—on time for once in her life—peered through the glass door, questioning whether she should come in.

Tammy waved her in. "My appointment's here," she said dismissing Lowell and his attitude.

Willette strolled in. Lowell got in the last word as he stomped out. "Give me a call when you change your mind. Maybe I'll be available."

"What was that all about?" Willette asked before the door shut behind him.

Tammy had known Willette all her life. Married to Bob Tidwell right after high school, Willette had three children, owned a nice house in a new subdivision on the outskirts of town, served as president of the PTA, taught Sunday school at the Baptist church and lived vicariously through Tammy.

Willette was sweet, a little naive and a lot nonjudgmental, so Tammy often supplied her with the ongoing dramas in her life, usually spicing them up for Willette's benefit.

"Lowell asked me out."

"Well, he didn't look happy."

"I turned him down."

Willette gaped. "Nobody turns Lowell down."

"Well, I just did." She wasn't going to argue the point that it was a crazy thing to do. "You've got a smudge of lipstick on your front tooth." Willette scrubbed at it with her finger.

"But he's..." Willette stumbled and Tammy came to her rescue.

"Hot?"

"Ye-ah. Definitely hot." Willette stared at her expectantly.

"What?" Tammy threw her hands up. "I didn't want to go out with him."

"You sure you're feeling okay today?"

"Never better." She'd always done what she wanted—the consequences be damned—and she didn't want to go out with Lowell. "Maybe I've been good for so long now, I've forgotten how to be bad."

"I don't think there's any danger of that happening," Willette giggled. "Hey, Bob heard the new vet's your neighbor."

News in Colthersville traveled faster than the speed of light. "Uh-huh."

"So, have you met him?"

"In the flesh." And that was truer than even Willette could handle.

"Come on. Tell all. What's he like?"

Tammy bit back a grin and pasted on a bland expression. This could be fun. "He sort of reminds me of a troll. Short, overweight, bad teeth, bad breath and a really bad disposition."

"Wouldn't you know it? Damn."

"Willette, you're a married woman." Tammy pretended shock.

"Yeah, but I'm not a dead woman. We've got two dogs, three cats and Kira talked her daddy into a guinea pig." Willette indulged in some eye-rolling on the guinea pig. Tammy couldn't blame her. "I spend a lot of time at the vet. I was hoping for eye candy. Why couldn't some hunky vet decide to move here instead of a troll—"

The bell on the door tinkled, interrupting Willette's good-natured bitching. Uh-oh, busted. None other than the troll in question, looking most untroll-like wearing jeans and a sweatshirt. His charming smile with its hint of uncertainty weakened her knees and heated her blood.

The awareness so conspicuously absent with Lowell earlier shivered through. Fine time for it to show up now. Shivering with Lowell would've been straightforward. She had the distinct feeling shivering with Niall would be a little more complicated.

"Hi. I thought this might be your place. I wanted to stop in and say thanks for the directions to the grocery store."

"No problem. I'm glad you're finding your way around town. Niall, this is Willette Tidwell. Willette, this is our new veterinarian, Dr. Niall Fortson."

Tammy had to hand it to Willette. She kept her jaw from dropping and instead put a friendly smile on her face as she shook his hand. "Welcome to Colthersville. I'm the keeper of two dogs, three cats and a guinea pig—I'm sure we'll be seeing a lot of you."

Niall smiled and Tammy suffered that same crazy weak-kneed response. "I look forward to it." He opened the door behind him. "I don't want to hold you ladies up. See you later."

Willette watched Niall walk away—no doubt admiring the impressive breadth of his shoulders, the fit of his jeans and the sheer sexy mass of him—and then turned to Tammy.

"You are so dead."

4

NIALL HELD ONTO the ladder's rung with one hand, leaned out and clipped the last of the Christmas lights on the upstairs gutter.

"Hi!"

Niall swayed and damn near embarrassed himself by falling off the ladder. Tammy crossed her lawn and stopped at his walkway.

"Hi." He hoped his grin wasn't as goofy as it felt. She was home from work. Not that he'd been watching for her to come home since late afternoon. Not that he'd gone out of his way to stop in and see her at work this morning. Not that he didn't know from their conversation last night that she was the last woman he should find so fascinating.

"Did you catch the Christmas fever?" she drawled with a naughty smile.

She was fever-inducing inspiration itself in her clingy red sweater, short black skirt and high-heeled boots. Just as knock-him-to-his-knees sexy as he remembered her from this morning. But it'd been Christmas she'd asked about.

"All the decorations inspired me," Niall admitted, climbing down the ladder. "The big tree in the town square. The decorations hanging from the lampposts. Makes you want to get into the spirit."

"Want me to turn them on for you?"

He nearly missed the last rung on the ladder. "Uh, sure. The outlet's on the porch. I'll get the ladder down."

She climbed the porch steps and picked up the extension cord. Her short skirt hiked up, offering a glimpse of rounded thighs above black stockings. A chain reaction shuddered through his body.

"I can't get it in. Hold on a minute. I think your prong is bent. There. That did it." *Thank God, he couldn't stand much more of her straightening his bent prong.* She glanced at him over her shoulder. "Are they turned on?"

Strands of multicolored lights spread Christmas cheer across his roof in the waning daylight. Both he and his lights were turned on. She was driving him out of his mind.

"Yes, that did it."

Tammy strolled down the steps and stood on the walkway, arms crossed beneath her chest. "Nice job. They look great."

Niall admired her admiring his lights, "They do, don't they?"

A sudden, awkward silence descended, the topic of Christmas decorations having played itself out but both of them reluctant to walk away.

"How was work?" Niall leaned against the porch rail and shoved his hands in his pockets, feeling like a fifteen-year-old dork instead of an accomplished man of thirty. Unfortunately he probably sounded that way as well. He wouldn't win any awards for brilliant conversation.

"It was great. I almost feel guilty calling it work. The only downside is my hands are tired by the end of the day." She held them out and flexed her fingers with their bright red nails. "And Saturdays are super-busy."

A minivan passed by. The driver waved and Niall waved back, although he didn't have a clue as to who it was.

"Dieter Fry," Tammy said. "He and his wife and their four kids live two streets over. They're friends with the Tidwells—you met Willette today."

"Right. She seemed like a nice lady."

"Willette's great." Tammy smiled.

"I hope it was okay that I stopped by."

"No problem. You're welcome anytime, unless the door to the massage room is closed and the In-Session sign is up." She hesitated for a moment and then seemed to make up her mind about something. "Stop by on Monday after work for a free massage. Consider it a professional welcome. You'll probably be ready for it by then, at the end of your first day." Her lips were the same shade of red as her sweater.

"That's very generous but the clinic doesn't close until six," he said.

"My last appointment is at five. That gives me time

to change the table and set up. Stop by around six forty-five."

She was proposing he take off his clothes and lie on a table, so she could touch him all over—well, almost all over. He was neither a saint nor stupid. "Twist my arm. I'll be there." He ran his thumb over a patch of rough wood on the handrail. "Would you like to come in for a drink? That is, if you don't have plans."

She was sexy, recently single and it was Saturday night. Righto.

She shifted her purse on her shoulder and climbed the stairs. "No plans. I'd love a drink."

"Good. Great. Come on in." Niall opened the door for her, his heart racing like an adolescent schoolboy in the throes of his first crush. Damn. His palms were sweaty.

Gigi immediately pranced over. "Hello, Your Badness," Tammy greeted her.

"Hope you don't mind wine out of a plastic cup. I still haven't unpacked." He gestured toward the boxes stacked in the living room. "I hate living out of boxes, but I hate unpacking even more."

"It's all about priorities. Christmas lights or unpacking? I think you made the right choice," Tammy teased as she sidestepped his golf clubs that hadn't made it into the dining room yet.

The sofa sat wedged between stacks of boxes. "I'm a little short on accommodations. If you won't be cold, we can fire up the chimenea on the back deck."

Tammy tucked her hair behind her right ear. "I've

been inside all day. I'd love to sit outside. Between my sweater and the fire, I should be warm enough."

"Good." Her incredible smile and her sweater were certainly keeping him warm. He opened the kitchen door for her.

"I love this room," she enthused as if it were a long-lost friend.

"Funky but fun?" Her enthusiasm was contagious.

"That's it." She turned to him. "It's impossible not to smile in here. It's therapeutic."

"Okay," he admitted, "the turquoise and yellow are growing on me."

Her smile broadened. "Ah, a convert. Now what can I do to help?"

"It should only take a minute or so for me to start the fire."

"I'm not in any hurry. Take as long as you need. Why don't I get the drinks ready while you get the fire going?" she offered.

"Good deal. There's a bottle of Pinot Grigio in the fridge if you like white wine. Or there's beer if you'd prefer."

Tammy dropped her head forward, massaged her nape and then rolled her head up in a slow, sinuous movement. "Chilled wine in front of a warm fire sounds heavenly. What can I get you?"

Her husky-voiced question fired his imagination and it didn't have anything to do with beer or wine.

"I'll take a glass of wine." Niall opened the door to the deck. "Plastic cups are in the cabinet above the

dishwasher. I'm pretty sure I threw the new cork-
screw up there beside them."

"I'll manage. You start the fire and I'll be right out."

He stepped into the descending twilight and closed
the door behind him. The smell of his freshly mowed
lawn permeated the crisp evening air.

Niall welcomed the rush of cool air against his
heated skin. He wanted Tammy with a fierceness that
left him breathless and disconcerted. He'd never felt
particularly fierce about anything or anyone before.

He pushed away from the door and laid the fire.
He'd situated the chimenea on the open corner of the
deck closest to Tammy's house and away from the
sprawling oak on the opposite corner.

Mia had bitched about him taking the chimenea, but
he'd stuck to his guns. It was the only thing they'd
bought together that he took when he left. He struck a
match and the kindling burst into flame. Sparks scattered out of the top and Niall poked at the wood until
the bigger pieces caught fire.

Carrying two cups and the opened bottle, Tammy
shouldered her way out the door.

"That's some fire there, Doc. You sure know how to
get it hot." She backed up to the fire, absorbing the
heat. She closed her eyes, a sensuous expression on
her face. "Ummm. It feels good."

He reminded himself to breathe. "It's seasoned, so
it'll burn hot and fast. I'll just have to stoke it more often."

"A little more work, but anything that feels this good is worth it."

Niall laughed from the sheer pleasure of the moment, the crisp night, the warm fire and her company. "Here." He pulled the wooden Adirondack love seat closer to the chimenea's metal grate. "I don't have anything more comfortable. Another vet school leftover."

"I didn't come over for the furniture." Even her laugh held a husky nuance that stoked the fire simmering inside him.

"That's a good thing." He took the wine bottle from her. The brief sweep of her fingers against his tracked heat along his nerve endings.

In the waning light, the pebbled tips of her breasts thrusts against her sweater front. "Is it too cold out here?"

She followed his gaze.

Christ, he could've just said, *I was staring at your chest and noticed...*

"No, I'm not cold." Her eyes held his as he poured wine into their cups. "I think it feels good. How about you, are you warm enough?"

He personally felt as if he was burning up with a fever from the inside out. "Yes."

She sank onto the love seat and stretched her legs out in front of her with sensual grace. She smiled up at him, "We can always share body heat if it gets chilly."

"Well, there's a plan." Niall folded himself into the other side of the love seat, placing the wine bottle on the deck floor. In the close confines, her body pressed against his from shoulder to thigh.

His heart thumped harder and faster. He hadn't tasted his wine yet and he already felt slightly drunk, intensely aroused by her body heat, her womanly fragrance and her close proximity.

She leaned back into the natural pitch of the chair and rested her head, revealing the delicate slant of her nose, the soft fullness of her cheek. "Ahhh. This was just what I needed, a toasty fire on a chilly night."

Her long, drawn out sigh did crazy things to his heartbeat. He should say something. Unfortunately, he seemed incapable of saying anything. Awareness wrapped around them, drawing them closer.

Niall knew they were going to take up where they'd left off last night. Anticipation was a powerful aphrodisiac.

Her cinnamon-scented perfume teased him, mingling with the fire's wood smoke. Tammy turned and looked at him without lifting her head, her mouth's fullness mere inches from his own, her eyes reflecting the fire's flickering flames. "Thanks for inviting me over."

Another fire, tendered by want, spread through him. "I'm glad you're here."

And he was. For the first time in months, he considered Mia's marriage refusal from a new perspective. If she hadn't turned him down, Tammy wouldn't be sharing a bottle of wine, a cozy fire and the close confines of lawn furniture with him.

Something inside him clicked as he let the past go, along with the anger and bitterness that had tinged him. He raised his cup in a toast. "To new beginnings."

She touched her cup to his, echoed his sentiment, and sipped. "Good wine. Not too sweet. Not too dry. You didn't have any trouble finding your way around today, did you?"

"No. You gave good directions." And she'd given him the right directions when she told him she was the town bad girl. At least two people had warned him about his thrice-divorced neighbor, her alcoholic father and her absentee mother. And he'd politely let them know he formed his own opinions of people based on his experience with them.

Tammy leaned forward. She picked a couple of pieces of paper up off the wood decking, and squinted at them. "What's this?"

He'd forgotten about those. They must've fallen out of his pocket when he'd built the fire. "Nothing important."

She glanced at them and then back at him. "I told you women would flock around you if you looked lost."

"Actually, I didn't have to look lost." Three different women had given him their name and number in the span of half an hour. Attractive women. He felt fairly certain he could've had a date with one of them tonight. Instead, he'd waited for Tammy to get home because none of those women intrigued him the way

Tammy did. Attraction had slammed him when he met her. He hadn't felt a remote flicker of interest in those women today.

"Merry Franklin. Barb Watson. Doris Turner." She read the names and then handed them to him. "That's quite a selection. Have you thought about which one you want to ask out?"

Was that a faint tightness edging her smile? He hoped so. His interest in her ran deep enough that he would resent her cheerfully passing him off to other women.

Across the darkening canvas of the autumn sky, stars began to appear. In the distance a car door slammed and children's high voices carried through the evening. Rather than intruding, the sounds accentuated their seclusion.

Her gaze reflected the heat that had simmered between them from the minute he'd met her.

"Yes, I've thought about which one I want to ask out." He drank from his cup, looking into her eyes, letting her see the desire for her that was burning him up. He put his cup on the deck and leaned forward, deliberately tossing the names and numbers into the chimenea. He sank back into the seat. The flames devoured the paper within seconds. "None of them."

"You're sure you wanted to do that?"

"Positive. *They* don't interest me."

"I'm not sure if that's a good thing or a bad thing."

"Neither am I."

She shifted on the hard wooden seat and her stockinged thigh slid against his leg. The sensation shook him, even through the layer of denim.

Tammy sipped her wine and looked at him. Her face was close enough that he could see a faint smattering of freckles across her nose in the firelight. "Why didn't you kiss me last night? You wanted to, didn't you?"

He trailed the back of his fingers against her cheek. Smooth satin. "I've never wanted to kiss a woman more than I wanted to kiss you last night. But I thought it was too soon after your divorce. I didn't want to make a pass at you when you'd been nice enough to invite me over." It sounded foolish when he tried to explain it, but she deserved the truth.

She turned her head and nuzzled his knuckles. "Hmm. So noble."

He didn't feel remotely noble now. Just very hungry for her. "Why did you kiss me last night?"

She reached up and stroked her fingertips across his jawline. "Because I wanted to."

Simple. Hedonistic. She feathered her fingers along his throat and he shuddered. "Hmm. So bold."

She stilled her hand against his neck, her scent weaving around him. "I am when I want something. Does it offend you?"

"No. I like it." Her lush mouth and body heat drew him like a moth to a flame.

She dropped her cup to the floor, spilling her wine. She didn't even glance in that direction. "Better to waste good wine than opportunity," she murmured, wrapping her arms around his neck.

Did she slide onto his lap or did he pull her there? He didn't know. It only mattered she was there.

He buried his hand in her hair, molding his fingers against her scalp, and gave in to the temptation that had plagued him all day. The taste of the chilled wine against her warm flesh scattered rational thought. Her lips clung to his, inviting him to drink deeper. She stroked her fingers against his neck, her touch trailing fire against his bare skin.

Hungry to taste more, he kissed from the edge of her mouth to the delicate line of her jaw. Her breath rasped in his ear in small gusts. Sliding his hand through her hair, he teased his tongue along the shell of her ear. The studs lining the delicate area played erotically against his tongue. Her sweater's softness cushioned his jaw.

Tammy twisted her head and rained slow, languid kisses along his jaw, exploring the sensitive area beneath his ear with her tongue. Niall dropped his head back, giving himself over to the sweet seduction of her mouth.

He swept his hand along the curve of her back and beneath her sweater's edge to the warm satin of her skin.

With a small moan she reclaimed his mouth, her tongue exploring him with bold sweeping strokes that throbbed through him. He groaned his pleasure and swept his tongue along the wet, slick heat of her mouth.

Without interrupting the kiss, she slid her leg over his, straddling him, her breasts pressed against his chest, her panty-covered sex riding his hard-on.

Frantic need replaced languor. Her mouth was hot and demanding. She buried her hands in his hair, her fingers against his scalp, holding him closer, a willing captive. He splayed his hands across the feminine curve of her back, pulling her tightly to him until her nipples stabbed against his chest. He slid his hands along her stockinged legs, stroking the nylon-clad length until he found the top of her thigh-highs. He groaned when he reached her bare thighs, then the plump rounded fullness of her satin-covered buttocks beneath the edge of her skirt. He gripped her, filled his hands with her cheeks, massaging them, squeezing them in a rhythm that matched the thrusts of their parrying tongues. Tugging her closer, Niall lost the last glimmer of reason when she surged against his erection.

Like a dash of cold water, barking erupted inside the house. Reluctantly she pulled her mouth away from his and he withdrew his hand from beneath her skirt. Her warm breath gusted against his throat in short, hard pants.

The barking grew louder and then faded. The dogs were racing between the front and back doors. "Someone's at the door."

"I think you're right."

He should go check. Instead he sat and stared at the picture she made with her mussed hair, kiss-swollen lips and her eyelids at an aroused half-mast. And quite frankly, he didn't have the strength of will to move her off his throbbing lap.

"I should go." Tammy stood and tugged her skirt down over her stockings. "I'll let myself out through the gate."

Niall passed an unsteady hand over his face. "I'm sorry about—"

"I'm not." She leaned forward, her hand on his chest, and pressed a hot, openmouthed kiss on his lips. She straightened and walked down the deck stairs. "You'd better go answer your door."

He stood, not sure what to say, except he knew he didn't want her to go. "Tammy..."

"Good night, Niall." The gate closed behind her.

Niall roused himself and grabbed a dish towel on his way through the kitchen. He could hardly open the door sporting a raging hard-on and whoever was there didn't seem inclined to go away. If this was some guy selling something, he was about to enact his own version of *Death of a Salesman*.

TIRED OF tossing and tangling in her sheets, Tammy abandoned her bed and tugged the down comforter off behind her. She wrapped herself in its warmth as she made her way through the dark house to the patio.

She hadn't been this unhinged by a kiss in, well, maybe ever. She flushed, simply remembering the feel of Niall's large hands on her butt, his hard length pressed between her aching thighs, his taste in her mouth, his scent on her skin.

And there was a whole lot more going on than him just being a convenient, warm body. Lowell was a convenient, warm body and she hadn't been interested. The chemistry hadn't been there—not like it was with Niall.

He was so different from any other man she'd ever known, with his quirky sense of honor that kept him from kissing her last night and had him apologizing tonight.

The way she saw it, there was only one sensible solution. Seduce him. She wanted him. He wanted her. Two consenting adults. She'd turned down Lowell. Niall had burned those phone numbers. Denial, rather than smothering the flame of desire, merely intensified it. Getting one another out of their systems would be the smart—and gratifying, if tonight was an accurate barometer—thing to do.

Stretching out on the chaise lounge, ensconced in the down comforter, Tammy welcomed the night's chilly embrace. She looked up. Framed by the towering outline of trees, myriad stars littered the inky black of the sky. She'd once told Olivia the best view at Pops's house was from the loft in the ramshackle barn out back. And it was. One of her favorite childhood memories was lying on her back, the sweet scent of musty hay surrounding her, peering up at the night sky through the missing tin in the roof.

Now she was content to sit here, reveling in her insignificance in the face of the universe. Aloneness, her one faithful companion since childhood, settled beside her.

Some folks, lacking a certain discernment, might mistake her aloneness for loneliness. She wasn't *lonely* a bit, but she couldn't recall a time when she hadn't been *alone.* Even with her three husbands and the men in between, her soul had remained untouched. There had been times, during and after sex, when she'd been achingly close to connecting to another human being, but ultimately there'd been no cigar.

At a younger age than she cared to remember, losing her virginity had been ridiculously easy. Naively, she'd thought to lose her aloneness at the same time, back when she still believed in the fiction of true love and soul mates. She smiled at the universe with only a tinge of melancholy. Her virginity was long gone and her aloneness had never left her side.

Without fanfare, a star arced across the sky's canvas, trailing light in its wake. Pure magic. She snuggled deeper into the comforter.

"Pretty awesome, wasn't it?" Niall's voice floated across the fence, under cover of darkness. It should've startled her. Oddly, it didn't. In a way she'd been expecting him.

"My mother used to say a shooting star was like sharing a piece of heaven." Of course, that was before her mother had dumped them all and left the family. She hadn't shared a shooting star with anyone since her mother. Until now. Until Niall. Gooseflesh danced across her skin at the realization.

"I'd go along with that." She heard his easy smile in the deep timbre of his voice. She envisioned his smile starting in his eyes and revealing the scar on his upper lip. "Looks like you have a better view than I do, less big trees in the way."

And it looked like he was angling for an invite. They had unfinished business. "Come on over. The gate's unlocked."

Anticipation trailed through her much like the shooting star as Niall's dark form moved silently along his fence line and entered her garden. What was it about this man that got under her skin? Surely, it was nothing that a little indulgence and seduction wouldn't take care of.

"It's dark over here." A faint breeze whispered through the trees, ruffling her hair and bearing his scent through the night shadows. A shiver that had nothing to do with the wind chased across her skin, tightening her nipples against her pajama's thick flannel.

"Watch your step. There's a slight step up to the stones."

Niall settled into the other chaise.

"How was Mavis's casserole?" She couldn't help teasing him. She'd checked out his visitor from the dark corner of her yard when she'd gone home. Mavis Taylor had stood on his front porch, her blue hair coiffed in neat curls, bearing a casserole dish like a virginal sacrifice. Mavis could, and would, talk for hours.

Niall groaned. "She's a very nice lady and I'm now fully acquainted with her family tree, including all her great-nieces and nephews and I fully regret that I wasn't here a month ago so that I could save her parakeet, Midge. But, she does make a mean chicken casserole. I told her I wouldn't eat if she didn't have some with me."

He was quite possibly the nicest man she'd ever met. "Mavis is a lonely little old lady. You probably made her week."

He shrugged. "She enjoyed talking. But that was fine. I don't particularly enjoy eating alone."

Tammy didn't mind a bit eating alone. There were a number of things she didn't mind doing alone, but there was one thing in particular she was tired of doing alone.

"Do you sit out here often at night?" he asked.

"Often enough. I love the night sky, the stars. I have ever since I was a little girl. Staring at the sky beats staring at four walls and a ceiling when you can't sleep."

"I had a little trouble sleeping myself."

Tammy smiled at the edge of frustration in his voice. She knew exactly what had put it there and she knew exactly how to take it away.

"It sounds like you have unresolved issues. Perhaps I could help."

"If I didn't know better, I'd think you were trying to seduce me."

"You would? Hmm." She stood, wrapped in her comforter. "If I were seducing you, it'd probably work better if I got a little closer." She moved behind his chaise and leaned forward, her breasts pressing against his shoulders. His sharp intake of breath hissed in the still night. "Just so I'd know what to look for, how would *you* seduce me?" she asked, hoping he'd play the game.

"If I was trying to seduce you, I'd do this." With his hand wrapped around her wrist, he pulled her around to stand beside him. He paused, offering her the opportunity to end this right now. He was twice her size and his huge hand swallowed her wrist, but his touch was loose and nonthreatening. She could've freed herself at any time. But the only thing she wanted to be free of was the ache inside.

The moment to walk away passed. He tugged her down. Tammy sank onto his lap and covered them with the comforter. Niall was hard and big in all the right places. Wide chest, broad shoulders, muscular arms, hard abs. Her buttocks fit snug against the vee of his thighs, her legs draped over his. She braced her hand against his chest. Even through the layer of his sweatshirt, his heart pounded against her fingertips. Her heart beat a matching rhythm.

Like a match to tinder, the attraction between them burst into flame. There was a time to take things slow, savor the moment. This wasn't one of them. It wasn't even a remote possibility. She'd been good for so long. Too long.

She reached up and pulled his mouth to hers. His lips met hers with an urgency that matched her own. Hot. Hard. Frantic.

Plunging tongues. Seeking hands. Urgent desire. Heat raced through her like a wildfire out of control. Moisture drenched her aching thighs. Cool air rushed against her heated flesh.

She craved him inside her.

"Niall, we have to do this now. Do you have..." Damn. She wasn't so carried away that she couldn't remember a condom. And she didn't have one with her. And what were the odds that her boy-next-door was carrying protection? There was always her house, but she wanted to do this here. Now. With the night sky above them.

"Yeah, move up a little bit," he instructed and dug in his front pocket. So, she'd been wrong about him. It was a nice surprise. They were on the same wavelength. She'd never been so happy to see a little plastic package.

In a rush, he unzipped his pants and removed them, along with his underwear. Tammy hopped on one foot at a time and yanked off her pajama bottoms.

It could've ruined the mood. It didn't. It was funny and sexy and she was totally turned on to be getting it on with Niall on her chaise lounge in the middle of a chilly night.

Niall laughed. "This is crazy."

"But you like it, don't you?" She straddled the chaise lounge, the night air cool against her wet heat. It only made her hotter.

"Oh, baby. Yeah. I like it a lot." Niall tugged her down to his lap, his hard, hair-roughed thighs arousingly masculine against her buttocks and thighs, his jutting erection just out of reach of the place where she most wanted to feel him.

He ripped open the condom package. She felt his hands shaking against her belly.

"Let me," she offered. She took it from him and rolled it over his shaft. He was hot, hard silk beneath her fingertips. And it might be dark, but there was nothing wrong with her sense of touch. He was... impressive.

She stroked the tight, heavy sacks at his base and he shuddered in her hand. He grasped her hips in his big hands, lifting her up, pulling her forward.

"Please...now...Tammy." His hoarse, nearly incoherent plea, sent her over the edge.

She plunged down. Yes. Exquisite.

"So good," Niall gasped, his breath coming in harsh pants that echoed hers. He slid his hands beneath her pajama top and cupped her breasts, rolling her nipples between his fingertips. The sensation arced through her body to where he was buried inside her.

"Oh, yes," she moaned and grasped his shoulders for support. She slid up his length and plunged back down while Niall played with her nipples, rolling, plucking the sensitive points.

She set the pace. Hard. Fast. Her bottom slapping against his thighs mingled with their harsh breathing, the sighs, the moans of encouragement that rose between them. He squeezed her breasts and fondled her nipples with a matching rhythm, his hips rising to meet hers.

Tammy threw her head back and looked at the stars. Each thrust, each plunge took her closer to joining the stars, to spinning into the universe.

She clenched her muscles tighter around him as the first wave of her orgasm washed through her.

"Come on, baby. I'm with you," Niall said and answered her spasm with his own.

He was with her when she soared and lost herself in the sensations that rocked her out of this world.

NIALL DIDN'T turn on the lights as he let himself back into his house. There'd been something magical, almost mystical about the experience he and Tammy had shared in the dark. He wasn't ready for the harsh light to dispel that.

New house. New vet practice. New lover. He had the distinct impression Tammy had thought they were a one-night stand. No way in hell. Instead of satisfying the hunger she aroused in him, their mind-blowing sex had merely intensified his craving. He wanted her again, but he also wanted to get to know her.

He stood by the edge of his bed and stripped. It'd taken a little persuasive talking on his part, but she'd agreed to dinner at his house tomorrow night.

He couldn't wait.

5

TAMMY LET HERSELF in Pops's front door and sought Olivia in the kitchen. They'd fallen into a routine of Sunday dinners at Pops's in a weird dysfunctional family effort to stick together. Occasionally Marty and his wife showed up. Usually, however, Marty was too hung over from the night before. She bet Marty was a no-show today.

Olivia sat at the worn Formica table peeling potatoes. "Hey. I wondered if you were coming."

Tammy dug into her purse for the blood pressure pills she'd picked up for Pops at the drugstore. She put them on the counter. "Remind me to remind him to take 'em. Okay?"

"Late night?" Olivia asked, eyeing her.

Tammy skirted the rip in the faded linoleum and plopped into a chair opposite Olivia. She picked the other peeler up off the table. "It was a slow morning."

She didn't add that she hadn't fallen asleep until the wee hours. She might've advertised to Olivia that she was looking for Mr. Right Now, but she was oddly reluctant to tell her he'd shown up. "Where are Pops and Luke?"

"They're working on the barn."

"Has Pops got his duct tape?" Pops used duct tape for repairs the way normal people used a hammer and nails.

"You know it." Olivia rolled her eyes.

"Luke's a good man to take on duct tape repairs with Pops."

Olivia shrugged. "He's adequate in a pinch." Total adoration shone in her eyes and belied her droll attitude.

Tammy eyed her pregnant sister's still-flat stomach and smirked. "Given your knocked-up state, I'd say you find him more than adequate. How're you feeling?"

"A little on the tired side."

"That's normal for now, isn't it?" She couldn't hide her panic. She couldn't bear it if something happened to Olivia. Even though it had taken a long time for them to become friends, she'd always loved her sister fiercely.

"Now you sound like Luke. Don't worry. The doctor says it's perfectly normal. I should have more energy in a month or so."

"Are you drinking your smoothies?"

"It's only been two days since I saw you," Olivia pointed out in amusement, "but, yes, I had one yesterday."

"Good. They should help with the energy. You told Pops?"

"We told him this morning."

"What'd he say?" Tammy scraped the skin from a

russet potato, praying he'd come through for Olivia.
Tammy hoped he'd been excited, but she really didn't
know how he'd react. She wanted to believe he'd
make a great grandfather, but he'd dropped the par-
enting ball countless times—mostly under the influ-
ence of Wild Turkey. Grandfather of the year wasn't a
given, either. Between Pops and the Rutledges, Luke's
snooty family who didn't quite approve of either Luke
or Olivia, the kid had slim pickings for grandparents.
Luckily, the tyke would have a hell of a set of parents.
And she'd try her damnedest in the aunt department.

"He said he was glad we were giving him a grand-
baby since you or Marty hadn't."

"Well, knock me down. Pops never showed remote
interest in grandchildren."

Olivia shrugged. "Go figure. He's really excited. I'm
so glad. I didn't know how he'd take it." She sniffled,
potato in hand, her eyes awash with unshed tears.
"Tammy, I want this so much for you."

Something akin to a lead brick settled in the pit of
Tammy's stomach. She tried using a bad joke to dis-
tract Olivia, who by this time had tears trickling down
her cheeks. "I'm glad you want it for me, but I've got
plenty of potatoes over here."

Even though Olivia giggled, her tears continued
and she stuck to her guns. "I want you to have a good
husband and a baby."

Once upon a time she'd wanted those things, as
well. When she still believed in princes and happily
ever after, before she'd had a taste of reality.

"I don't want another husband. And we should all be grateful I didn't drag a bunch of kids with me from marriage to marriage. Thank God and birth control pills I'm not tracking down child support checks every month."

"Why didn't you ever have a child?" Olivia asked, tears streaming down her face.

She and Olivia had never been close enough for Olivia to ask before, and in the last year, as they'd become friends, it had never come up. Chances are she wouldn't have answered it, anyway. But how did you tell your hormonal, weeping sister it was none of her business?

Unfortunately, Tammy didn't know how. Which left the option of offering her an answer. Rattled by Olivia's uncharacteristic weepiness, she blurted, "I was scared."

Now that was a hell of a thing to up and say. Olivia abandoned all pretense of peeling potatoes and stared across the Formica expanse and sniffled, her gray eyes watery, awaiting an explanation.

Tammy pushed away from the table and walked to the counter. Olivia had cried for a year after Martha Rae, their mother, had left. Tammy, who ached so bad inside she hadn't been able to cry, had figured Olivia cried enough for the both of them. And then one day Olivia stopped crying. Twenty-three years ago could've been yesterday because, God in Heaven, Tammy still couldn't stand to see her little sister in tears, hormonal or otherwise. She tore a paper towel off the roll and handed it to Olivia. Olivia dutifully dabbed at her eyes.

Tammy turned her back to Olivia and braced her hands on the sink, staring out the window with its cracked pane. "I was terrible at being a mom to you after Martha Rae left."

"You weren't—"

She looked over her shoulder and interrupted Olivia's denial. "Olivia."

"Okay, so you were. But you were just a kid, for goodness' sake. Very few nine-year-olds make good moms."

That had been the most abysmal period of her life. She'd hated everything and everyone. Hated her mom for leaving, hated her family for driving Martha Rae away and most especially hated the pity in people's eyes when they looked at her. She'd been so angry, it'd been easy to build a bad reputation that kept everyone and their pity at bay.

"And..." And she'd grown up to be afraid she couldn't love a child enough for it to love her in return. God knows, she hadn't loved her mother enough for Martha Rae to stick around. And she hadn't loved any of her husbands enough to keep them at home. As much as she wanted to explain all this to Olivia, the words wouldn't come. She couldn't lay her soul that naked to anyone, even her sister. "And now you're going to have one that I can spoil rotten." She sucked in a deep breath and firmly closed that particular discussion. "What's up at the library?"

Olivia, very wisely, let it drop. "The Coulther County Regional Library is rocking. We were swamped yesterday at storytime, which was a good thing. The number of kids has almost doubled. They love the new addition."

"Kids in a castle turret. What's not to love? It's very cool." Tammy was pretty proud of all the changes her sister had made at the library. Olivia had almost single-handedly raised the money to build the library's new addition.

"Willette brought Kira to storytime yesterday. She said she'd met your new neighbor."

Tammy didn't care for that speculative gleam in Olivia's eyes. They'd moved from one dangerous subject to another in record time. "Yep."

"She said he was...how did she put it? Oh, yeah, eye candy."

"If you like that sort." Tammy shrugged and began to rinse the potatoes in the sink.

"And what sort is that?" Olivia joined her at the sink.

This was the downside to being friends with Olivia. She felt perfectly justified in minding Tammy's business.

"Sort of serious. Sort of quiet. Sort of boy-next-door." Sort of sexy. Sort of an incredible lover. And there was no way she was sharing that with Olivia. Let Olivia even catch a scent in the wind that she and Niall had this "thing" between them, and Olivia, who could be frighteningly determined when she set her mind to something, would be absolutely relentless.

Tammy didn't want to find herself the focus of that kind of determination. And Olivia had already told her she wanted to find her a husband. She'd consider Niall prime husband and father-to-be material. Actually, he was, if you were looking for that kind of thing.

"Hmm. Willette said he stopped by your place to see you." Her casual tone didn't fool Tammy for a minute.

Tammy held up her hand. "You're barking up the wrong tree, sister. And it wasn't to see me, it was to thank me. Being the good neighbor that I am, I gave him directions to the grocery store. That's all. Not my type."

Liar. Liar. Her conscience smote her. When you factored in his wanting to settle down, that made it only half a lie, she argued in return.

"If you say so." Olivia neither looked nor sounded convinced. "She also said Lowell asked you out and you turned him down."

"Willette covered it all, didn't she?"

"Pretty much. So, I guess Lowell's not a Mr. Right Now candidate?"

Olivia was going somewhere with this and Tammy was pretty sure she wasn't going to like it. "Nope, not today."

"Well, I'm glad to hear it cause I don't like Lowell

and you never know when Mr. Right Now might turn into Mr. Right.''

Now that was a totally scary thought.

SWEAT DAMPENED Niall's T-shirt and trickled down his neck, despite the cool day. For approximately the hundredth time over the course of his five-mile run, Niall mentally listed through all the reasons he should stay away from Tammy.

She was complicated. She was his neighbor. She came with a lot of baggage. She had a really bad attitude about marriage. She didn't particularly like children or animals. Her reputation was just as bad as she'd claimed.

Attractive women without half of the above strikes against them would be delighted to go out with him.

And for approximately the hundredth time, all those reasons failed to sway him in light of one indisputable fact. He wanted her. Again. Something about her touched him, beckoned him. It was more than just the sex—which had been pretty incredible. Despite her in-your-face, what-you-see-is-what-you-get bravado, her underlying guardedness intrigued him.

He turned onto his street and kicked into high gear, sprinting from the corner to his driveway. He immediately noticed Tammy had returned. Her car hadn't been there when he'd started his run.

Sweat-soaked, heart pounding, he slowed to a walk when he turned into his driveway.

"Hi." Her head popped up from the back of the plastic manger scene in her yard. She waved a lightbulb. "Baby Jesus burned out."

"Can't have Baby Jesus burnout."

"Not if I can help it." Tammy laughed as she stood up, brushing grass from the knees of her jeans. "I didn't realize you were a runner. How far do you go?"

"Five miles a couple of times a week. It builds good stamina," he said.

A wicked glint lit her eyes as she looked him over from head to toe and back again. "Stamina's important."

"I work hard at going the distance." Her face flushed and she moistened her lips with her tongue. She was enjoying this conversation as much as he was. "Maybe you could try it with me sometimes."

"I'd have to turn down that offer. I'm not a runner, wrong body type. I prefer dancing and yoga. The yoga keeps everything limber, and dancing is quite a work-out—releases lots of pent-up energy."

He knew firsthand just how limber she could be and he had no doubt she'd turn dancing into an erotic experience. Now there was a stimulating idea. Too stimulating for the driveway at dusk.

"Maybe you could try a dance workout with me one day." Tammy peered at him from beneath her lashes, Salome issuing an invitation.

"Sure." He'd agree to almost anything when she looked at him like that, but him dancing was in the same time frame as hell freezing over. Niall's two left feet were something of a Fortson family joke.

"Are we still on for dinner? I've worked up quite an appetite." Her smile took his breath.

"I've got just the thing for you. I think you'll like what I've prepared." He was damn nervous about it, actually.

"I'm sure it'll be very satisfying. When should I come?" she asked, her voice dropping a seductive note.

He was well on his way to a raging erection and running shorts weren't exactly discreet. "Give me half an hour to clean up."

"What can I bring?"

"I've got it covered. Just bring yourself."

"I can manage that." He'd walked about halfway to his front door when she called out his name. He half turned. "Yeah?"

Devilment danced in her blue eyes.

"Nice shorts."

6

NIALL SHOVED his shirttail in his jeans and opened the door.

"You got a Christmas tree," she exclaimed, skipping the conventional greeting. "I saw it as I came up the front steps."

Niall grinned, pleased she'd noticed, pleased by her enthusiasm and generally pleased she was at his door. "I sure did. Come on in."

She stepped past him, the brush of her arm against his and the waft of her scent rekindling the banked fires from earlier.

"Did you bring your tree with you from your other house?"

"No. I braved the shoppers and bought it today. It came with the lights and I don't care if it doesn't have ornaments. I just had to have a tree. Even as often as we moved when I was a kid, we always had a Christmas tree."

"It complements the packing boxes," she razzed him. "Are you a procrastinator by nature or is it just these boxes you can't seem to get to?"

"Unfortunately, they may still be here six months from now. I hate packing and unpacking. Maybe because I did so much of it when I was growing up. I got to the point where I just lived out of my suitcase and boxes. It was easier that way."

"Yeah, but this is different, isn't it? You're here to stay," she pointed out.

"Yeah, I guess you're right." Despite the words and his intent, he realized he still hadn't made the mental transition.

Tex and Lolita blinked at them from the back of the sofa. Gigi and Memphis lay curled together on a dog bed near the Christmas tree, both sacked out. Tammy gestured toward the dogs. "What's up with them?"

"They exhausted themselves this afternoon chasing Frisbees and squirrels. Gigi has this thing where she jumps up and catches the Frisbee in midair."

"Oh, I bet that's cute."

"It is funny. And she must've leaped for it at least a hundred times."

"Poor Tiny Mite, no wonder she's tired." She caught herself in midcroon, a sheepish expression on her face.

Well, what do you know? Ms. Cooper wasn't as immune to pets as she pretended. "It takes a lot to wear Gigi out. Tex and Lolita, on the other hand, exhaust themselves just walking from the food bowl to the couch. Come on." Niall took her by the arm to lead her to the kitchen.

With that one touch, mirth gave way to something far more potent. Heat spiraled through him as he led her down the hallway.

Niall stopped short of the kitchen door and turned to face her. "Okay, close your eyes."

Tammy blinked but her eyes remained open. "What?"

"It's a surprise. Close your eyes. I promise I won't let you run into the wall or anything."

"How do I know I can trust you?" Wariness lurked beneath her banter.

"You don't. Sometimes you have to take a leap of faith." He didn't think that was an easy task for her.

She lowered her lids, her lashes dark crescents fanning over her cheeks. She wrapped her hands around his forearms, her touch eliciting tingles against his bare skin. Grasping her elbows, he walked backward as he led her just inside the kitchen. He stepped and released her to close the door behind her.

"You can look now." Christ. He was as nervous as a schoolboy.

She opened her eyes and glanced around the room. Cautious delight and wonder washed her face. "You did this for me?"

He nodded. "This afternoon." He'd bought a dozen candles, a blanket and a Christmas cactus, and created a picnic in the center of his kitchen. Space hadn't been an issue since he didn't have a stick of kitchen furniture. "You said you liked this room."

She looked away from him. "This is probably one of the nicest things anyone has ever done for me. Why would you do this?" she asked, her voice thick.

"Because I wanted to see you smile." He touched

her shoulder with a tentative hand. She still wouldn't look at him. "And it's too cold to sit outside, even with the chimenea."

"It's…"

She sounded close to tears and the last thing he'd wanted was to make her cry.

He looked around at candles glowing on the countertops and the floor. "Were you going to say it's a fire hazard? That's why I had the door closed. To keep out the animals."

She drew a deep breath and turned to him. "Actually, I was going to say it's very thoughtful. Are you always so romantic?"

He heaved a silent sigh, relieved she didn't just think he was stupid. A man never knew how a woman would interpret things, or at least this man didn't. And Mia had sworn he didn't have a romantic bone in his body.

"Never. I'm glad you like it," he said.

"I do. Very much."

"I thought I'd make salmon steaks for dinner."

"That sounds good."

"I should get started," he said.

"Okay."

He fully intended to walk over to the fridge and pull out the salmon steaks and ask her what she'd done with her day. Instead, he stood rooted to the spot, close enough to inhale her scent and absorb her warmth. And somehow, instead, he said, "I thought about you all day."

"I thought about you, too." Her husky drawl drew him a step closer.

"You did?" He reached out and tucked her hair behind her ear. He trailed a finger along the soft down of her neck, eliciting a quiver.

"Yes. You should be going out to dinner with one of those women whose number you tossed in the chimenea last night instead of planning a picnic for me." Despite her words, she splayed her hands across his chest, her touch branding him through his shirt.

"I know. They don't have your baggage." He stroked along the line of her collarbone to the wildly beating pulse at the base of her throat.

"Or three ex-husbands." She dipped her head and pressed an openmouthed kiss to the back of his hand. God, he'd never known that was an erogenous zone before. Maybe it only was with her.

"Yeah. Them, too." He could barely breathe. The touch of her skin against his, her fragrance, the heat in her eyes damn near left him dizzy with want.

She feathered her fingers up his neck and cupped his jaw in her hands, brushing her thumb against the scar lining his upper lip. "I should be doing this with Lowell."

"I don't think so." He flicked his tongue against her thumb. On her indrawn breath, he slid his hands down her side and grasped her by her waist, hoisting her up to the countertop. Her eyes widened with a start of surprise and then darkened. "Who the hell is Lowell?"

She spread her legs and tugged him into the vee of her body. "Nobody important right now."

"Good answer." His erection nestled against her and he pulsed within the confines of his jeans. They both were still fully clothed, they hadn't even kissed and he was damn near ready to explode.

She moaned deep in her throat and rocked against him, wrapping her legs around the backs of his thighs, pulling his throbbing hardness against her.

"Niall." His name came out as a sigh. She tunneled her fingers through his hair, pulled him closer and latched her mouth onto his like a woman in desperate need, as if he alone supplied something she couldn't live without.

He explored the hot, sweet moistness of her mouth. Her moan reverberated against his tongue, fueling his hunger. When she arched into his hands with a desperation that matched his own, he ran his hands across the top of her breasts exposing her plunging, scooped neckline. The blouse's crushed velvet didn't compare to the warm satin of her breasts.

Niall rimmed the lace edge of her bra where it met her pillowy flesh, skimming her stiff nipples. He wrenched his mouth from hers and rained kisses along her neck, freeing her breasts from her bra, weighing their fullness, rimming her hardened tips with his fingers without actually touching them.

Above his head, her breath came in sharp, harsh pants, punctuated by low moans, the sounds of her pleasure notching his heat up to a flammable level.

She leaned back on the counter, bracing herself with her arms behind her. "Touch me."

He spread a series of tantalizing, taunting kisses across the top of her breasts, still not touching her dark crests. "Like that?"

"More." Half order, half plea. Total turn-on.

He laved first one pebbled tip with his tongue and then the other. She arched toward him. He looked up at her. "Is that what you wanted?"

"Take the whole thing in your mouth," she rasped, her eyes glittering with a heat he'd put there.

Slowly, deliberately, he drew her engorged tip into his mouth and suckled her. Tugging her deeper, harder.

"Yes. Oh, that's it." Her cry of satisfaction became a mewl in the back of her throat that nearly undid him. The sounds she made fed his passion.

"What about this side?" He turned his attention to her other puckered crest. He pulled back and looked at her, thoroughly aroused by the sight. Sitting on the counter, her bare flesh damp and glistening from his mouth, Tammy radiated sensuality.

Niall cupped both breasts in his hands and drew them together. Angling her nipples together, he circled each aureole with the tip of his tongue and then lapped at the hardened tips.

"Oh. Niall."

He blew gently on them, fascinated as they hardened into even tighter buds. He repeated his dance of licking and blowing, her cries as exciting as her taste. Her scent, hers alone, enveloped him.

Pressing her breasts closer together, he drew both her nipples into his mouth at once, abrading them lightly with his teeth, filling his mouth with her, tormenting her. Finally, he released her, consumed by a craving far beyond physical.

He drank in the sight of her. She appeared every inch the wanton, sitting atop the counter, legs sprawled, breasts bared, eyes glittering.

"I have never wanted a woman the way that I want you." His voice rang harsh in the candlelit room. God help him, but Mia had never driven him out of his mind the way Tammy did.

"Forbidden fruit?" With her full, ripe breasts and plum-hued nipples, she was dangerously close with her analogy. He almost missed the shadow in her eye and the faint cynical edge to her voice.

He cupped her cheek in his palm. Part of him wanted to deny it, part of him wanted that simple explanation for his overwhelming attraction to her. "I don't know. Maybe." He dropped his hand to his side.

She covered herself and slid to her feet.

He wasn't great at figuring out women, but he felt pretty damn sure he'd just given the wrong answer.

"I KNOW THIS is bad timing but we both need to be clear on where we stand." They needed rules of engagement.

Niall's expression and his crossed arms said her timing left a lot to be desired. "Okay."

"I like you, Niall." She glanced at Niall from beneath her lashes. She appreciated his easy, dry humor, his thoughtful, romantic gestures, and the honesty in his soulful dark eyes.

He raised his brows. "I assumed *that* when we had mind-blowing sex last night. And by the way, I like you, too."

She glanced at his erection tenting the front of his trousers and she was terribly aware of the moisture pooled between her thighs. "I know you do."

She needed to say this. *Maybe as much for herself as for him.*

"I like you and I find you very sexy, but I don't want another relationship. I like living alone. I'm focused on my job and getting my life together. I don't need any emotional complications."

He just stood there, his dark eyes unreadable, arms crossed, and she shifted, suddenly a little less sure of herself. But the only way to go was forward. "I just wanted you to know you don't have to worry about me reading too much into this." She pointed at his picnic. "I know you're looking to settle down here in Colthersville and I want you to know I don't want to complicate that for you."

"It sounds like you've got this all figured out."

Actually, she was just sort of winging it as she went. "I've had too many relationships that die a slow death, where, in the end, you can hardly remember any of the good stuff because things have gotten so bad."

Recognition flashed across his face. He knew the death throes of a relationship. "Been there. Done that."

Tammy nodded. "That's why an affair is perfect. Short, brief, exciting. No strings attached. No pretense. No seeing what tomorrow will bring."

"But what if we aren't ready for it to end?"

"That's why we set the rules now and stick to them. Things get awkward, messy, when expectations change. This way we both get what we want and no one gets hurt because we both know what to expect up front."

"Intellectually it makes sense. I'm not so sure about emotionally." In part because he wasn't sure that he knew what he wanted.

"We like one another. We're definitely attracted to one another. And we can both get what we want without any games."

He traced a vein on the back of her hand. "So, let's discuss the rules of engagement."

She caught his hand in hers and brought it to her mouth. Her warm breath stirred against the back of his hand, and her lips lightly brushed his knuckles.

"Two weeks. That way you don't have to worry about what to get me for Christmas," she said, interjecting a little humor. "We can keep it quiet and private. I'll be your fling before you find your nice girl and settle down."

"If you're my bad-girl fling, what am I to you?"

Tammy slid her arms around his neck and leaned into him, rubbing her pelvis against the hard line of his penis. "You're my Mr. Right Now."

He closed the gap between them, a wicked smile curling his lips and lighting his eyes. Her heart somersaulted. "I was hoping you'd say that."

He cupped her shoulders with his hands and drew her to him. She wound her arms around his neck and threaded her fingers through the hair that brushed past his collar. The heat of his skin, the faint scent of deodorant and soap, the silky texture of his hair, sent shivers through her.

Her eyes drifted shut and she sighed as he leaned down and feathered butterfly kisses along her temple and eyelids with exquisite care. How could a man who aroused such a depth of passion in her feel so safe?

"You are so beautiful," he whispered, his breath warm against her closed lids. His words and his touch melted her like a piece of chocolate left too long in the sun's heat. She'd heard the empty phrase before, but when Niall uttered the words, they lost their emptiness.

Tammy leaned into him.

"Do you want to go upstairs?" he asked.

She opened her eyes. "Beds are highly overrated, especially when there's such a lovely picnic in this room."

She withdrew her hands from his neck and sank to

the blanket. She leaned back, bracing herself on her arms. It had been dark on her patio last night. She'd felt every inch of him, but today she was ready for the full visual experience.

Niall tugged his shirt free of his jeans, slowly pulled it over his head, and tossed it to the floor.

Broad shoulders, thick chest and honest-to-God delineations of his abs. A sprinkle of dark brown hair across his chest narrowed to a line down his flat belly, and disappeared beneath the edge of his jeans. Well-muscled arms and sexy forearms. She wasn't sure what it was that made them so sexy, but they were. Dear God, she was glad she was already flat on her back.

"Absolutely awesome." She hadn't exactly meant to speak the words aloud.

Niall smiled. "I'm glad the Nautilus machine wasn't a waste of money."

"Oh, honey, you've put it to good use. Definitely no waste of money there." It was true. Why not tell him?

"Hold that thought." He stepped out of his shoes and shoved them aside.

Tammy stared. She had a bad case of lust-itis when even his feet turned her on. "You have the sexiest feet. I thought so when you answered the door after your shower, the first time I dropped by."

"Do you have a thing for feet?"

"Not until now." She returned his grin and motioned for him to continue disrobing. "Please, don't let me stop what you were doing."

He undid his belt. Then his jeans button. He slid down his zipper. Tammy's heart pounded like a runaway train. Niall stepped out of the jeans. Muscular, hair-roughened legs and black boxer briefs with a bulge that portended good things to come.

"You can change your mind, you know." He stood at the edge of the blanket, big, aroused and hers for the next two weeks. Anticipation coiled inside her.

"You've got to be kidding. If I changed my mind, I would've lost my mind."

"I meant about the bed." Niall knelt at her feet. "I fully intend for you to lose your mind."

His dark promise unleashed a new torrent of longing. Wet need pooled between her thighs. "You do? Do you want to share this plan with me?"

"It's fairly simple. Not too complicated. Pretty straightforward."

"Are you going to show me or tell me?"

"I'm all up for both. First I'm going to take your clothes off. Then I'm going to kiss every delicious inch of you."

Ye gods. Tammy suffered an attack of insecurity. While she'd been so busy behaving, she'd gotten lazy in the exercise department. And fat. Even though Niall had seen her au natural, it wasn't the same as having him visit that particular site up close and personal. This was a really bad time to realize she shouldn't have slacked on the crunches.

She swallowed her insecurities. He looked fairly enthusiastic—she glanced at his bulging black briefs—

make that extremely enthusiastic—at the prospect of getting her naked again, and, what the heck, she was what she was. She sucked in a deep breath and went for it. "That sounds like an efficient plan. How can I help implement it?"

"Lie back and enjoy." He tugged off her shoes and tossed them aside, his dark eyes intent, despite his sexy banter. "I want to make love to you all night long."

Anticipation coiled tight inside her. "Ah. That stamina issue."

"Yeah. It keeps coming up."

"So, I see. That's quite some issue you have there."

"Perhaps you could help me deal with it."

"It would be my pleasure."

Niall reached for the snap on her jeans, his hands big and broad with a masculine dusting of dark hair. Slowly, deliberately, he released the snap and drew down her zipper, the drag of his hands against her bare skin and panties setting her afire.

"Before I take these off, I've got to do this. I've wanted to since the first time I saw you." Niall bent his dark head and swept his tongue across the ring piercing her belly button. The wet heat of his tongue against her stomach left her twice as hot and wet between her thighs.

"Oh, honey, you have the sexiest stomach. There's something about that navel ring that makes me hot."

"Your appreciation makes me pretty hot myself."

"I know."

"You do?"

With his chin, he nudged against her open jeans and the satin of her panties, a wicked grin on his face. "It's your scent, your own special perfume. It's intoxicating."

She'd never made love to a man who talked so much. It was surprisingly uninhibited and incredibly inspiring.

Niall inched her jeans down over her hips, killing her composure with his deliberateness.

Tammy lifted her hips so he could continue. "Umm, I bet you unwrap Christmas and birthday presents without tearing the paper, don't you?"

"I like to take my time. Savor the anticipation. It heightens the pleasure when you actually get to the present."

He tossed her jeans aside and drew her to her knees.

"Let me," she said, taking over. She grasped the hem of her shirt and pulled it up over her head. His eyes darkened and his breathing took on a harsh tone. She wet her lips with her tongue and he clenched his jaw. Good. She unhooked the front clasp on her bra and slowly tugged it open, thrusting her breasts forward and her shoulders back as she took it off.

All teasing left his demeanor. Intensity glittered in his dark eyes and marked the rigid lines of his body. "This is the way you were meant to be. Naked in candlelight. I wish I were an artist so I could paint you like this. You are the most beautiful sight I've ever seen."

She'd had sex numerous times, most recently with him, last night. But now she felt like a virgin. Without even touching her, Niall was making love to her. With his eyes, his voice, his words. She'd known it would be different with him, but she hadn't known it would be like this.

His eyes stripped her of all pretense, all defense and looked inside her, to her core, her essence. It was both frightening and exhilarating to feel so exposed, so open to another person.

All her instincts of self-preservation, survival and denial screamed for her to get up and run like hell.

And she might've done it. She might've actually made it off the blanket and out of the room if Niall hadn't reached out and touched her.

SHE SAT BEFORE HIM, totally naked. Her skin gleamed like molten gold as candlelight danced erotically across her bare skin. For one moment she'd let down her guard and her face had been an open door to what was deep inside. In that instant, he'd glimpsed Tammy's heart. Her softness. Her strength. Her fear. She was Mother Earth, Aphrodite and Eve all rolled into one. The longing to make her his own consumed him.

He reached out and traced the rounded curve of her shoulder. She wasn't some mythical creature. Rather, she was a warm, pliant flesh-and-blood woman. He trailed his fingertips along one breast, over her nipple, lower still over her belly until he reached the soft curls between her thighs. She dropped her head back with a soft sigh.

He slipped his fingers through her curls and found her slick folds.

Her moan and her sweet heat nearly sent him over the edge. She was so hot. So wet. So ready. All he could think about was pleasing her. Slowly, he slid a finger into her tight sheath and was rewarded by her husky cry. This time he slid two fingers into her and she lifted her hips to take his fingers deeper inside, a soft mewling coming from her throat.

"More?" he asked, barely recognizing the guttural voice as his own as he withdrew his fingers.

She grasped his wrist and drew his hand to her lips. With a carnal smile she took his glistening fingers into her mouth and suckled them. Pulling them back out, she slowly, deliberately tongued his fingers. She released his hand and uttered two words. "Yes. More."

It was the most intensely erotic experience he'd ever had. The desire to please her became a fever in his blood. He pulled her mouth to his. His tongue delved her moist heat, tasting her, while he slid three fingers into her tight, silken channel. He absorbed her open-mouthed moan as he slid his fingers out and then in again. Her cries intensified, vibrating erotically against his tongue as he plunged his fingers faster and deeper into her wet heat until she screamed her release into his mouth, her nails biting into his arm, her sweet essence drenching his hand.

In the sudden, abrupt stillness, her breath mingling

with his own, Niall felt Tammy's heartbeat against his fingertips still inside her, as if they were one. He felt almost hungover. He'd been totally out of control.

She reached between them and touched him, stroking the full length of him through the cotton. A shudder wracked him.

Her eyes at half-mast, she murmured, "Those black briefs are incredibly sexy, but it's time for them to go."

He levered himself on one elbow and pulled them down and off with his other hand. His sex sprang free, at full attention.

She closed her eyes briefly and opened them again, desire and hunger in their depths, a naughty smile on her face. "Oh, my."

He wouldn't have been a normal guy if he hadn't been pleased by her reaction. And he was very pleased indeed by the heat in her eyes and the appreciation in her smile. He wasn't setting any world records in the size department, but no one called him Tiny Tim, either. "It's all proportionate. I'm a big guy. I'd have looked pretty silly with a little...well, little equipment."

She stroked the length of him, her touch tightening his balls. "There's nothing silly here."

"I'm glad you're not laughing. It'd be sort of tough on the ego."

"I'm definitely not laughing." She squeezed gently but firmly and he pulsed against her palm. "You know that plan you had earlier?"

Plan? He wasn't too terribly sure of his own name

right now after what they'd just done and with her touching him like that. "Hmm?"

She circled him with her fingers and stroked up and down in a slow rhythm that nearly unhinged him. "Niall?"

Yeah, that was it. That was his name. "Umm?"

"Remember that part of your plan where you were going to kiss me all over? Save that thought. I can't wait that long. I'm ready again."

He was damn sure he wasn't going to be able to wait, either. Especially if she kept this up. He ought to stop her, but it felt so incredibly good. Just a little bit longer. "I don't think I can wait for that, either."

"I want you in me this time." Raw desire underscored her words.

"That's just where I want to be." He reached behind him and pulled his wallet out of his jeans. His hands shook as he removed a condom.

She lay back and opened herself to him. He wanted her to feel as frantic as she'd made him. He slid between her slick folds but didn't enter her, rubbing his shaft against her. Once. Twice. By the third time her breath was coming in short, hard gasps. She thrust her hips up and wrapped her legs around him.

"Now," she ordered, eyes closed, lips parted.

They might've agreed to an affair, but he was more than just a warm male body. He wasn't going to obligingly do his part while she shut herself off in her own private world. He wanted all of her, not just her pertinent body parts.

"Open your eyes. Look at me. Let's go there together. Me and you."

She opened her eyes and locked her gaze on him. Slowly he entered her, inch by sweet inch.

Dear God, she was so wet. So tight. So hot. Finally, he was buried in her. Fully engaged. Her muscles clenched around him. "That feels so good."

"Yes."

He pulled out slowly and then entered her again in one long, slow stroke. "And that feels even better."

"Yes."

He reached between them and rubbed her sensitive nub. She cried out, her pleasure mingling with the harsh rasp of his breathing. He rubbed her as he drove deeper and harder into her.

They became one in a rhythm and he lost himself in the depths of her eyes, the hot sheath of her body, the sound of her passion.

Her cries grew sharper, more frantic as they approached a place without thought, only sensation and emotion.

Together they fell over the edge, soaring, spiraling, caught up in something more intense than physical release. For a man who'd traveled the world over, never rooted anywhere, Niall had found his place. He'd come home.

TAMMY ROLLED onto her side, positive she'd never felt so good in her life. "That was quite an appetizer. But now I'm starving."

Niall wore a dazed expression, one arm beneath his head. "I'll get up in just a minute."

She lightly scraped her nail along his muscular thigh. "You're quite impressive when you're up."

"I'm glad you approve. Let me slip on my clothes and I'll make dinner."

"Don't." She stilled him with her fingers against his sheathed penis.

Niall laughed. "I thought you were hungry."

"I am. But the view will be much better if you don't dress."

"You've got a deal, on one condition. You leave yours off as well."

"Not a problem. I like being naked."

"It suits you."

She'd never had a man prepare a meal for her in the buff. Actually, she couldn't remember a man ever cooking for her before. And she'd never made love on a blanket in the middle of a kitchen floor, either.

He levered himself up and excused himself. He returned in record time. "A salmon filet and salad coming up. I have to warn you, I'm not a gourmet cook."

"That's fine. I'm not a gourmet kind of gal. And regardless of how you cook, you certainly present a gourmet view."

"You certainly know how to stroke my ego— among other things."

She reached for the "other thing" playfully and he dodged her. "You'd better concentrate on my ego if you want to eat tonight."

"Spoilsport."

"Vixen."

"Watch your tongue. You know how that affects me."

"Behave."

"Okay. Let me find some totally nonvixenish topic of conversation." She eyed him seriously. "You must be very excited about starting at the vet clinic tomorrow. I know how I felt the day I opened my business."

"It's something I've wanted for a very long time."

"Do you always get what you want?" About the time the question came out of her mouth, she remembered Mia, who was sitting on a nice sofa somewhere in Oklahoma City. "Sorry, I forgot about your ex."

"No problem. I forgot about her, too. I guess I get what I want, most of the time. Perseverance and determination make a lot of things happen. And I can be very determined." He glanced at her pointedly. "As for Mia, I think that worked out for the best. I have a newfound perspective on things. Apparently Mia knew something I didn't."

Unless she was totally clueless, he was telling her he was glad things hadn't worked out with Mia so he could be with her now. Tammy was both flattered and a little frightened. In response, she did what she did best when emotions or relationships got too close for comfort, she changed the subject rather than deal with it.

"What? Is this a man admitting he was wrong?"

"You don't think very highly of us men, do you?"

"It's just the voice of experience. But I do think highly of you." She laughed as she said it, but she realized it was true. She not only liked Niall, she respected him.

For the first time in as long as she could remember, it was fiercely important to her what someone else thought of her.

When her mother abandoned them, Tammy'd found people's pity intolerable. She'd take scorn over pity any day. She'd created and worn her bad reputation like a coat of armor. She'd deluded herself that she didn't care what people thought. The truth was, she'd felt so insecure, so inadequate, it had mattered too much.

She wasn't courting Niall's scorn or his pity, but she wanted him to know the truth. And for the first time in a long time, she felt as if Niall was someone she could trust with the truth. The thought that Dr. Schill was likely to give Niall his version of the Thanksgiving incident bothered her immensely.

"When I was married to Allen, Dr. Schill's son, we'd spend Thanksgiving Day at his parents'. It was the second year we were married. Allen and Margaret, his mother, had taken the dogs for a walk before dinner. I was in the kitchen and Ted came in. He cornered me next to the pantry and touched me. I was his son's wife and he fondled me." She shuddered at the memory of his hands on her breasts.

"The bastard."

Niall should've looked slightly ridiculous swearing

and wielding a knife, butt-ass naked in his yellow and turquoise kitchen. Instead, he was about as close to a knight as Tammy had ever encountered. "You believe me?" God, please don't let her cry. She swallowed the lump in the back of her throat.

"Of course I believe you. Why wouldn't I?"

"Allen didn't." She stared at the blanket, pleating it between her fingers.

"What?"

His angry question snapped her head up. Tension corded his muscles.

"He said I had misunderstood his father or else I'd led him to believe I wanted him to touch me." It shamed her to admit it aloud. Her own husband hadn't thought enough of her to believe her, to believe *in* her.

"Sounds like being a bastard runs in the family." Good answer.

She smoothed out the crease in the blanket. "I've never told anyone other than Allen. But I wanted you to know the truth, in case Ted makes some snide comment about me. I know how men can be."

"Not all men are like that." He stared into her eyes, piercing her with his gaze, the same way he had earlier. Intimate, probing, knowing. "I'm glad you felt like telling me, but I would've known anyway."

That was, without a doubt, the nicest thing anyone had ever said to her. Niall, who barely knew her, believed her without hesitation or indictment. Relief washed through her. Embarrassment and self-consciousness at getting carried away and revealing so much of herself quickly followed.

"It's not a big deal. I just wanted you to know. Something smells delicious."

Niall's look told her she was perfectly transparent in her diversionary tactics. "It's my premarinated fish. It'll be served tonight with my prewashed, precut bagged salad."

"I should've brought dessert."

His look scorched her.

"You did."

7

"MRS. MACALLISTER'S CAT was the last case today, sir." Trena, by far the most efficient of the three office technicians, stuck her head in his office.

"Thanks. I'll finish up these notes and call it a day." It had been a great first day. He couldn't think of a better ending to it than Tammy's massage and whatever might follow.

"Sir?" Niall glanced up again. Trena still stood in his doorway. "If you wouldn't mind, we had a stray dropped off today. I thought you might want to take a look at her."

Niall checked his watch. Six-fifteen. He was due at Tammy's office in fifteen minutes. "Where is she?"

Trena smiled, her relief evident. "She's in the back. I'll bring her up to Room 3."

"Good. I'll meet you there."

Niall looked up Tammy's office number and dialed. She answered on the second ring. Her smokey voice knotted his gut.

"Hi, Tammy. It's Niall. I've got one more case. If you can't wait, I understand." He'd understand, but he'd be sorely disappointed.

"Busy day?"

"Busy, but good. Dealing with the owners wears you out more than dealing with the animals."

"Hmm. Sounds as if you need a little TLC." His body quickened in anticipation. "How long do you think you'll be?"

"Probably another quarter hour or so."

"I'll still be here. The Closed sign is up and the front lights are off, but I'll leave the door unlocked. Just lock it behind you."

"I'll be there as soon as I can."

"No rush. I'll wait."

Niall hung up. Add patient and understanding to sexy and funny and sweet beneath her bad-girl persona.

Niall walked down the hall and firmly pushed Tammy from his mind.

"In the four years I've been here, we've never had a greyhound come through here before. She's in pretty rough shape. Jeb Barnwell found her beneath the underpass on the way out of town," Trena said, moving aside so he could take a good look at the animal.

A painfully thin brindle female cowered next to the exam table, visibly shaking. Keeping his voice to a low, soothing croon, Niall approached the dog. "Hi, girl. Let's check you out. Okay?" He squatted and methodically ran through the exam. "Pupils are dilated but then she's scared. Lots of tartar build-up on her teeth, but her gums are good. Ears just need a good cleaning. Heart sounds okay. CRT is less than one.

Based on her skin turgor, she's mildly dehydrated. Probably seven to ten pounds underweight, too."

"It's hard to tell with her shaking, but she limps on the rear right leg," Trena told him.

Niall felt again. "Doesn't feel like anything's broken. She may have pulled something. According to her ear tattoo, she's three and a half years old. I bet she was retired from the track, got adopted and then somehow became separated from her owners. How'd we get her instead of the pound?" He was curious.

"Jeb has a soft spot for dogs and he figured we'd have better luck getting her back to her owners or finding a new home for her. He didn't want to take a chance on her being put to sleep. He said he'd foot the bill for her."

"Jeb sounds like a good man."

"Yes, sir, he is."

"Is she microchipped?"

"No, sir. We checked."

"Go ahead and do a fecal. Check her for heartworm. Make sure she has a good dinner. The National Greyhound Association in Kansas should have information on her. We can call tomorrow."

Although judging from the way she cowered, he suspected she'd been mistreated by whomever had her before. He hated turning innocent animals back over to unkind owners. It was one of the toughest parts of his job. "Do you know much about these dogs?"

"No, sir. They're beautiful but, like I said, we've never had one in here before."

"Elevate her food bowl and even if you have to feed her a little at a time, don't let her gobble her food." He stroked the dog's long, elegant neck.

"Yes, sir. And thank you for staying to look at her."

"I'm sure Dr. Schill would've done the same."

Despite her eyebrows hiking up her forehead, she replied blandly, "Yes, sir."

First thing in the morning, Schill had introduced him to the staff he hadn't met on his previous visit, wished him well, and taken off to uphold his end of a foursome on the golf course. And that had suited Niall just fine since he'd wanted to knock the hell out of the bastard for feeling up his daughter-in-law several years ago. Niall considered it a bonus Schill would be gone within the next three months.

Thank God he'd bought the practice and not a partnership.

"*Would* Dr. Schill have stayed to look at her?" He rubbed his hand down the dog's spine and her trembling subsided a bit.

Trena squared her shoulders. "No, sir."

"Then you'll find two things will be different from now on, Trena."

"Yes, sir?"

"First, I will examine any animal that needs looking at regardless of the time on the clock. It's my job and there's no emergency clinic in town. So, if an animal needs to be seen, you let me know. Got that?"

"Yes, sir." Trena smiled as she picked up the dog's leash.

"And the second thing...don't call me sir."

"Yes...okay." Her smile blossomed into a full-fledged grin on her way out the room.

Niall washed up and finished his notes for the day. On his way to the back door, Trena looked up from her stool at the lab station.

"It's nice to have you here...." Trena said from behind him, catching herself before she tacked on the *sir*.

"It's nice to be here. I think we're going to work well together. Are you almost through?" Trena was about the same age as his sister Lydia and he hated to think of her going into a dark parking lot on her own.

"I wanted to run her fecal and I thought I'd clean her up a bit." Trena wore a sheepish expression. "Don't worry, I'm off the clock and I'll lock up when I leave."

Niall shrugged into his jacket. "I'm not worried about whether you're on the clock. Just be careful going out into a dark parking lot."

Trena burst out laughing and then caught herself. "I'm sorry, Dr. Fortson. I appreciate your concern, but this isn't Oklahoma City. I know almost everyone here and my brother's the deputy sheriff."

He laughed at himself, feeling slightly foolish. "Sorry. I still haven't made the transition to a small town, I guess. Good night."

The door clicked behind him, cutting off her good-night. It took some getting used to the familiarity found within a small town after the anonymity that even a midsized city afforded. That was one of the things that had appealed to him about living in a small town—there were no strangers here. Another aspect of small-town living, he noted with a slight smile, was that everything closed early. It was only seven o'clock but the streets were already deserted.

Niall enjoyed the walk across the street and down the sidewalk in the evening's bracing chill. Christmas decorations adorned every lamppost and lights twinkled among the trees in the town's center.

Although Tammy's waiting room was dark, a lit Christmas tree in her window welcomed him.

He let himself in and locked the door behind him, the jangle of the bell startling in the quiet. An exotic scent hung in the air. A light glimmered beneath the edge of the door across the room. Niall skirted the furniture, crossed the dark waiting room and opened the door. He stepped in and closed the door behind him.

Low soothing music—maybe a South American pan flute—and dim lighting filled the room with tranquility. Tammy, wearing a white lab coat over her clothes, stood on the other side of a sheet-draped table. She looked beautiful and professional and almost as nervous as he felt. His heart did slow somersault inside his chest. For want of something to do besides stare at her like some besotted veterinarian who'd made a deal not to get emotionally involved when it might already be too late to uphold the bargain, he glanced around the small room.

Sand-colored walls. Instructional posters delineating the muscular and nervous system. On one wall a bookshelf held stacks of fresh, folded white towels, candles, a compact disc player and several jars of oils and ointments. "This is very nice. Tranquil."

"Thanks. I'm glad you could make it. Hectic first day?"

Niall shrugged. "It was good. It's a good clinic and the staff is great. Ted took off to play golf."

"I don't want you to dislike him on my behalf. That's not why I told you that. He has a reputation for being a very good vet."

She was a remarkable woman. Schill had treated her like dirt but she seemed genuinely concerned she'd adversely affected Niall and Ted's working relationship. "I understand. But I'll be watching my back until he leaves. A man without honor is a man without honor."

"I've never met a man like you before." The wariness in her eyes reminded him of the stray he'd examined earlier.

"That's just what I say about you. But not the man part."

Tammy laughed. "Are you ready to get started?"

"In a minute. First, I'd like a kiss." Her boldness must be rubbing off.

"That's nice, Dr. Fortson, but I don't mix business and pleasure. You'll just have to wait for that kiss." Her eyes smiled along with her delectable mouth, but she was quite serious. He respected that she didn't mess around when it came to her work. "Now, you can step into the other room and take off your clothes. The underwear is optional."

"You are a wicked woman."

"Do you really think so? Thank you. I try my best. Now, if you'll quit whining and take your clothes off, I'll work your kinks out."

"Oh, honey, I love it when you're assertive. It's very sexy. You don't happen to have black leather on underneath that, do you?" Niall surprised himself at his playfulness.

"That's for me to know and you to find out. Later." She opened the door behind her. "When you're ready, lie down on the table and cover yourself with the sheet. I'll give you a few minutes before I come back in." She closed the door behind her.

Niall stepped into the changing room and undressed. He'd already unwound a great deal flirting with Tammy. He left his boxers on. Given the effect Tammy had on him, he'd prefer to have something extra between him and the sheet if he embarrassed himself with a hard-on.

He stretched out on the warm table and settled between the crisp, fresh sheets with a sigh. Hell, it already felt good and she hadn't even touched him. "I'm ready."

She walked in with a pleasant, businesslike smile. "Let me tell you a little about what we're going to do, so you won't be surprised by anything." While she talked, she placed a warm blanket over him, covering him from his toes to his armpits. Amazing how good soft sheets and a warm blanket felt. "I'm going to start with your head and work my way down. A lot of therapists start with you facedown but I prefer to end the massage that way. If anything feels uncomfortable, let me know. Otherwise, just lie back and enjoy it."

Tammy positioned herself on a stool behind his head and Niall closed his eyes, fully willing to give himself over to the sensations. The unperfumed scent of her skin wafted around him, along with the soothing music as she kneaded the back of his neck and up into his skull.

She paused and he smelled another fragrance. "Is there any particular area that's been uncomfortable or where you've had a problem?" Her disembodied voice floated behind him, low and soothing.

"Not really."

"Good. I'm going to use a menthol, eucalyptus and camphor lotion now." Her hands, warm and slick and fragrant, glided over his shoulders. Gooseflesh prickled along his skin as she rubbed and kneaded.

At first, Niall was aware of every movement. Tammy massaged past his thigh area and he heaved a mental sigh of relief. Now that he'd managed not to embarrass himself with a woody, he relaxed.

Tammy had him roll over to his stomach, facedown on the table. Her touch, the music and the warm table lulled him into a state of total relaxation. He drifted somewhere outside of consciousness.

"Niall," her voice was a distant murmur. "I'm going to leave the room. When you sit up, do it slowly. How do you feel?"

He roused himself from a near-stupor state of relaxation and turned his head to look at her. "Incredible. That's how I feel."

"I'm glad you enjoyed it."

He rose up slowly and turned over on the table, sitting up, the sheet draping over his lap. He was beyond relaxed but he was still a man and she was still the woman he wanted. "Is the business part over?"

"Not until you put your clothes back on."

"Damn." He was only half kidding.

"Meet me in my office when you're dressed." She pointed to the room beyond another door. Promise lingered in her sultry smile.

Niall beat a path to the dressing room. He couldn't remember ever feeling this good outside of sex. And that had been with Tammy as well. She just seemed to generate good feelings.

Her massage had left him with an amazing sense of well-being, physically and mentally. It hadn't just felt good, it had a therapeutic quality.

An image flashed through his mind of the shaking, limping stray he'd examined. He wished he could make the poor animal feel as good as he felt.

He buckled his belt, an idea taking hold in his mind. Tammy definitely had a healing, relaxing touch. Not content to wait until he put on his shoes and socks to share his idea with her, he threw open the dressing room door. "Tammy."

"Yes?"

He couldn't offer the greyhound a therapeutic massage, but he certainly knew someone who could.

"There's something I'd really like for you to do for me."

"I'M TELLING YOU, I don't know how to do that." Despite her protest, she followed Niall into the veterinary clinic. While she argued with Niall, she looked around. Gingham curtains hung at the windows and a cat and dog border topped soothing blue walls. Margaret Schill must've decorated the clinic. Her former mother-in-law had been very fond of gingham. Doors flanked each side of the receptionist's desk. One nook of the waiting room displayed a variety of pet foods and products. It was cheery and pleasant, except for the antiseptic smell.

"She's just a dog. Massage her like you did me. It was great and I really think it would help her."

"But I don't know anything about animals."

"Their muscular-skeletal system isn't that different from ours, except they walk on four feet. Come on. Just try it. It can't hurt to try." He caught her hands in his. "There's something special in your touch." Niall's dark-eyed entreaty was hard to resist.

"You're just saying that because—"

"Because it's true."

"And here I was thinking it was because you wanted your own way." She knew a line when she heard one.

He raised her hands to his lips and pressed a light kiss on the back of them. "Please."

Maybe she didn't know a line when she heard one. Or maybe she was just a pushover. But either way, he was right—what could it hurt to try? And it wasn't as if anyone was asking her to take the dog home. She just had to massage it. "Okay. Where is she?"

It was worth agreeing just to see the smile on Niall's face. "Back here. In the kennel." Clasping her hand in his, he pulled her along behind him, through an exam room into a long hall that ran the length of the building.

Before they reached the kennel door, barking assaulted them.

Tammy had never set foot in a veterinary clinic. She'd grown up so poor, veterinary care hadn't been an option. This was all new territory for her. "Are all of the dogs back here sick? They don't sound sick. They just sound noisy."

Niall raised his voice to be heard over the melee.

"They're not all necessarily sick, some are recovering. The really noisy kennel is through the other door where we keep the boarders."

Niall opened the door and the barking, no longer muffled by a door and walls, assaulted her. "Wait here and I'll bring her out."

Niall led out a tall, thin dog with a mottle-colored coat and haunting eyes. Gracie's eyes. Despite her obvious half-starved state, she was strikingly elegant. "Let's take her to my office." He nodded his head toward the opposite end of the hall, "Dr. Schill's office is down there."

"You don't share an office?"

"Until he officially retires in three months, it's his office. I believe mine was a supply closet before I came."

Tammy thought Niall was only teasing but his office certainly was small, with a banged-up wood desk which would qualify as an antique in a couple of years, and two chairs, one behind the desk, the other in front of it.

After taking off the leash, Niall stepped away. Tammy looked at the dog, who stood stock still and regarded her with an unblinking, wary stare.

"She won't run away or jump on me?"

"Only if a bunny or some other small furry animal runs past. Then she'd be hell-bent to chase it. But other than that, no." Tammy caught a glint in his eye. Was he laughing at her?

"Will she bite?"

"She won't bite or snap. I doubt if she'll even bark. She'll just stand there."

"What about that shaking?" It was a bit unnerving to see the poor animal trembling so.

"She's scared. I suspect she's been through a lot. That's why I thought you could help."

Tammy drew a deep breath and approached the dog. The dog stared straight ahead, even though she shook harder when Tammy stood by her side. Cautiously, carefully, she ran her hand along the dog's long neck. A shudder passed through the animal.

"It's okay, girl. I'm not going to hurt you. I'm going to try not to hurt you, anyway." Tammy pitched her voice low. She murmured nonsensical reassurances as she rotated the pads of her fingers against the dog's thick shoulder muscles. Gradually, as Tammy continued to talk and stroke, the dog's shaking subsided. By the time she worked her way to the massive thigh muscles the greyhound leaned against Tammy's leg. The dog wasn't exactly relaxed but she'd stopped her terrible shaking.

"I knew it would work," Niall said.

His voice startled her. "I forgot you were here."

"That's flattering," he said with an elated grin. "I knew you could help her."

She didn't even try to check her answering grin. No one had ever shown or professed such abiding faith in her as Niall. A sense of well-being and accomplishment coursed through her. "She does seem much calmer."

Tammy sat in the worn chair in front of Niall's desk. The dog followed, much less wary, and stood before her. The greyhound nudged Tammy with her long nose and eyed her expectantly. "What?" Tammy looked at Niall for help. "What does she want?"

"Maybe more of the same?" he suggested with a smile. "It looks as if she liked your massage." Niall reattached the dog's leash. He paused in the doorway. "Let me put her in the kennel and I'll be right back."

The dog looked back at her. For an instant Tammy glimpsed something familiar in the dog's eyes. "Night, girl."

The dog whined in response.

"You seem to have an addictive touch. I may be suffering from withdrawal myself."

Warmth flooded her. When he used that low, sexy tone, he could report on the weather and it would still turn her insides to mush. It wasn't so much what he said as the way he said it. "Hmm. I hate to hear of anyone suffering, especially if I can help."

"Ah, you're in a unique position. You're the cause and the cure. Are you through with business for the day?"

"I believe I am. Why do you ask?" She knew exactly what he had in mind.

"Because I'm definitely ready to move on to pleasure."

8

TAMMY WAITED for Niall with a surprise she knew he'd appreciate. She'd hovered on the brink of sexual arousal all day, anticipating his touch, his smell, his taste.

His footfall sounded in the hallway and she canted her legs open, giving him an unencumbered view beneath her short skirt.

Niall stopped in the doorway.

"I took them off at my office, while you were getting dressed, to make the transition from business to pleasure."

"I wholly approve of your methodology." He leaned against the door frame with a nonchalance belied by his heavy-lidded gaze.

"I thought you might."

"Have you ever made love in a veterinarian's office?" He could've been asking if she preferred peas or broccoli.

"No. It's at the top of my to-do list tonight. What about you? Have you ever made love in a veterinarian's office?" She shouldn't have asked, but the answer was suddenly terribly important to her. Even though it went against her philosophy of not getting too involved, she didn't want to be just another "sex-at-the-office" experience for him.

"No. I was never interested until now, but it's suddenly come up. Maybe we can help one another reach our goals."

"I'm counting on it." Tension mounted inside her and coiled between them in the small office.

"Open your legs wider. I just want to look at you."

The hard edge to his command further inflamed her. She felt ripe. Swollen. Wet.

"I read an article that says men are visually stimulated, but I wasn't sure so I thought I'd conduct my own study. Since you have a scientific background..."

"If it's in the name of science, I could be persuaded to help."

She unbuttoned her blouse. The cool air glided over her breasts, a stark contrast to his hot gaze. "Do you find this stimulating?"

"Moderately so."

She skimmed her hands over her breasts, and without unhooking her bra, lifted them over the edge. She cupped them in her hands and brushed her thumbs against her nipples. "Purely from a scientific view, how do you find this?"

"Stimulating. Definitely stimulating."

She slid her hands down her sides, across the tops of her thighs. With her fingers splayed against her inner thighs, she slid her legs further apart.

"Yes," Niall uttered, down to one-word affirmations.

Tammy wasn't sure how much speech she was capable of, either. She rubbed slow, tight circles against the sensitive flesh of her inner thighs, delighting in the increasing heat in his eyes. With tantalizing deliberation she touched herself, slipping her finger inside, between her hot, slick folds.

Her eyes never leaving his, she brought her finger to her lips and slid it into her mouth.

His gasp echoed the rigid lines of his body. He crossed the room in two strides, his eyes glowing with intent. "From a purely scientific point of view, I'm stimulated off the chart. And I've got hard evidence to prove it."

"So I see."

He pulled her to her feet and she willingly met him more than halfway, their mouths melding together in a frenzy of anticipation and passion. His lips were hot and eager and she strained against him, welcoming the hard lines of his body, the thrust of his arousal against her.

She wrapped her arms around his neck and he slid his hands up the backs of her thighs, then beneath her skirt. He kneaded her bare bottom with his large hands, pulling her more firmly against his erection while his lips marauded hers. She moaned into his mouth with need.

She was on fire for him and him alone. Being with Niall was unlike any other experience. It was as if she'd found what she didn't even know she'd been searching for. He tapped into and aroused her to depths of passion she'd never known before, but beneath it all was a sense of security, of safety, she'd never felt with anyone. And not only did he want her—lots of men had—but he seemed to admire and respect her, and that was a new experience.

Lost in the sensations of his taste and touch and heat, she didn't realize they'd moved until she felt the press of the wood desk against her bare thighs. Niall wrenched his mouth away from hers and shoved aside the papers, then lifted her to sit on the desktop. The battered wood was cool beneath her bare thighs and buttocks, an arousing contrast to the heat consuming her.

Niall dropped to his knees before her and whispered his hands across the back of her thighs. Anticipation gripped her. She curled her fingers around the desk's edge. Bracing his hands against her thighs, he parted her with his thumbs and gazed at her. "You are exquisite. Absolutely beautiful."

Her breath hitched in her throat and her muscles clenched.

Dipping his dark head, he kissed her, intimately, deeply. Waves of pleasure rippled through her. Already aroused, she gave in to the orgasm that seemed to start at her core. Niall gripped her thighs as she thrashed, his mouth bringing pleasure so relentless, so piercing, she felt as if she were shattering into a million pieces.

Still caught up in the throes of one of the most intense orgasms of her life, she met Niall's gaze as he looked at her from between her thighs, his bottomless black eyes reflecting arousal. Hunger. Intent.

He stood. Tammy slid to her feet and leaned against the desk for support. Despite the orgasm that had just devastated her, she craved the feel of Niall inside her. "Tell me you have a condom." Her voice was as unsteady as her legs.

Niall reached into his pocket. "Yes."

Within seconds he was sheathed, both of them still clothed. He turned her around and pulled her back against him, his arm a steel band beneath her breasts. His warm breath, redolent of her scent, gusted against her neck and sent shivers along her spine. His erection teased her from behind. In between hot, sucking kisses along her nape, he commanded, "Tell me what you want."

She gripped the edge of the desk and looked over her shoulder at him. "I want you. Inside me." Small pants punctuated her words.

"When?" His harsh, urgent whisper intensified her ache.

She ground back into him and he pulsed against her in response. "Now."

He bent her forward, over his desk. And then he was in her, filling her, stretching her, connecting with her in a primal way, engaging her whole being, body and soul.

"Every time I sit at this desk, I'll remember your sweet taste, our scent. I'll remember being deep inside you—as if I'm touching your soul. I'll remember your breasts against my desk, the sound of your voice in this room when you come."

With each thrust he plunged deeper, harder, finding an achingly sensitive spot. Coupled with his words, she found it almost unbearable.

A part of her wanted to cry out for him to stop, unsure she could bear it, uncertain there'd be anything left of her afterward. Another portion of her felt as if she'd die if he stopped. Like a piece of flotsam caught up in a storm of epic proportions, she felt the waves break over her, sweeping her under, carrying her along, heedless of her will.

Spent, she lay draped across the desk, Niall braced over her, his last spasm echoing inside her. Her thundering heartbeat reverberated in her head.

"I've never...that was..." Niall said.

He verged on incoherence, but she knew what he meant. "I know. Me, too."

Niall withdrew. It was as if he took a part of her with him. He sank into the chair and pulled Tammy onto his lap.

With an unsteady hand, he brushed her hair away from her face and pressed a kiss to her forehead. "Are you okay? I lose control when I'm with you."

"That was...you know..." Every word that came to mind seemed inadequate. "Don't ruin it by apologizing." She cupped his jaw. "You weren't the only one out of control."

And that was all it was, she reassured herself. She'd been swept up in a physical reaction stronger than any she'd experienced before. Nothing more. Nothing less.

An odd buzzing sounded in the distance. Niall stood, almost dumping her in the process. He righted her. "Sorry. We better think fast, because someone just came in."

Tammy tugged down her skirt and tried to quell the panic rising within her. She didn't care what people thought about her, but it wouldn't do Niall any good to get caught boffing her in his office. She inhaled deep calming breaths, resolved to do the finest acting job of her life to protect his reputation.

"WHAT ARE YOU DOING HERE, Dr. Fortson? I saw your car was still out back. Is everything okay?"

Niall and Tammy met Trena in the hallway. Niall was damn glad they'd made it out of the office before Trena made it in. The scent of their lovemaking permeated the air. In about two seconds flat she'd figure out the new doctor had just shagged his neighbor.

Niall stalled for time. "Trena, do you know Tammy? She's my next-door neighbor."

"Sure. How are you, Tammy?" Trena looked at Niall. "Tammy used to do my nails but, thank God, she gave that up because she gives the best massage in three counties."

"Thanks, Trena. How's the shoulder?" Tammy appeared relaxed and composed. Incredible. His brain still felt like mush.

Trena lifted her left shoulder and winced. "Still a little twingy."

"Call me tomorrow and I'll get you in on Wednesday or Thursday."

"That's why Tammy's here—not because of your appointment," Niall babbled, "but because of Tammy's massage skills. I asked her to work with the greyhound and the results were impressive. She was much more confident and her limp was much less noticeable by the end of the massage."

"That's excellent. I've got some news, too. After you left, I called the National Greyhound Association since they're a couple of hours behind us. The dog's name is Fair Game. She retired from a Florida track six months ago and was adopted by a G. Burns. I tried the phone number they gave me and it's been disconnected. The real bummer though is she tested positive for heartworm."

"Damn," Niall swore.

"I know," said Trena.

"Well, *I* don't know. What does that mean?" Tammy asked.

"It means she has to be treated for heartworm. Some dogs make it. Some don't."

"Oh." Tammy looked like she wanted to cry.

An idea took hold. He'd seen the bond, felt the connection between woman and dog. "I've got an idea. Hear me out," he said to Tammy and Trena. "I've taken a lot of ribbing from some of my colleagues, but I believe in a holistic approach to healing. It's more than just physical. She obviously connected with you, Tammy. If you could foster her through the heartworm treatment, she'd stand a much better chance of recovery."

"No," Tammy said.

"Yes," Trena enthused.

"I don't know anything about dogs."

"It's easy and the main thing you need to know is that a little TLC could mean the difference between life and death to her. She's going to be tired so a house without any other pets would be ideal."

"Do you really think so?" Tammy said slowly.

"I do."

"He's right, Tammy," Trena said.

"How long would it be? Before she'd be out of the woods?"

"It takes five months for her to fully recover from the heartworm, but if she makes it the first month, then she'll be fine," Niall said.

"It would make it much easier to find her a home," Trena added.

"But what if she...dies?"

"That's a possibility. But she's young and appears healthy other than that. Animals are similar to people—the will to live goes a long way."

"I wouldn't have to keep her five months?"

"No. Just until she pulls through this or we find her a home."

Tammy closed her eyes and rubbed her forehead, as if warding off a headache. She dropped her hand and looked back and forth between Niall and Trena, resigned, definitely wary. "Okay. I'll take her."

"Can you take her tonight?" Trena pushed.

"I don't—"

"The sooner the better." He looked at Trena. "Unless you're in a hurry to get home, could you get together some food and a crate?"

"No problem. Max is bowling tonight with his league." Trena started down the hall and stopped to look back at Tammy. "I think it's wonderful you're doing this."

She didn't seem to notice the tight edge to Tammy's smile. Humming beneath her breath, Trena hurried down the hall and into the dog room to get everything ready.

"I'll be right next door. There's nothing to it," Niall reassured her. He thought Tammy needed the dog probably more than the dog needed Tammy. But, being a wise man and not wanting her to withhold sex or something equally drastic by being pissed off at him, he kept that particular thought to himself.

"She'd be better off with you. You take her," Tammy suggested.

"She's a sight hound and she may not be small-animal friendly."

"What does that mean?"

"It means that it's been bred in her for a couple of thousand years to chase small, furry things. Some dogs have a higher prey drive than others."

"Oh, God. She'd eat Gigi and the cats?"

"Nah. She'd just grab them by the back and toss them around until their necks snapped."

"That's horrible."

Niall shrugged. "Don't hold it against the dog. It's her nature. But you can see why I can't take her."

Maybe he was laying it on a little thick and maybe he was playing on the fact that he knew Tammy liked Gigi whether she'd admit it or not, but all was fair in love and war and sometimes the stuff in between.

"I had a dog once," she said baldly, her back to him as she stared at a feline food analysis chart posted on the wall.

Maybe he'd known it all along. He'd certainly sensed there was something going on with her and animals. They liked her and she kept her distance. "What happened?"

"Gracie was my best friend. After my mother left, Pops came home drunk one night. He didn't mean to let her out of the house. A car hit her."

Losing a pet was hard. He reached over and touched her stiff shoulder. "I'm sorry."

Tammy turned to look at him, her blue eyes pools of misery. "She didn't die right away. Pops was passed out and even if he'd been sober, we wouldn't have had money for the vet. My brother offered to...put her out of her misery but I couldn't let him. Instead I just held her. It took her two hours to die."

He could only repeat himself. "I'm so sorry." Shit. It was one thing to lose a pet; it was a different matter to watch it suffer for several hours. And he'd all but forced her to take the greyhound. "Listen, forget it. You don't have to take the dog. We'll work something else out."

Tammy drew a deep breath, squared her shoulders, and turned to face him. "No. I'll take her. I couldn't do anything to help Gracie. But I can do something to help this dog. I can't—I won't love her like I did Gracie, but I can help her." She looked down at the tile floor and then back up at him. "She's got Gracie's eyes." She uttered the last sentence so softly, he barely heard her.

"Are you sure? You really don't have to do this," Niall argued, hating the sadness in her eyes, feeling responsible for opening an old wound.

"I think I do."

Niall didn't know what to say and Trena saved him from a response when she came out from the back with the trembling dog, a bag of food and two stainless steel bowls. "Here she is. Ready to go."

The dog saw Tammy and stopped shaking. Trena looked from the dog to Tammy and dropped the leash. Without any prompting the dog walked over to Tammy, looking up at her with her sad, solemn eyes.

"What's her name again?" Tammy asked.

"Her track name was Fair Game." The dog didn't even look in Trena's direction when she heard the name. "But she doesn't seem to respond to that. You can name her."

"No. I don't need to name her," Tammy said with a quiet detachment.

The dog pressed her head to Tammy's hand. "She definitely likes you. And lucky for you I gave her a bath earlier. She was pretty stinky."

"Trena, if you'll go over how to feed her and how often, I'll load the crate in my Explorer." Niall looked at Tammy. "I've got the cargo area. I can take her in my truck and drop her off at your house, okay?"

He held his breath. Would she back out? She wanted to—trepidation was all over her face. The dog nudged her once again, taking the decision out of her hands. "Okay. You bring her in your truck."

They were making progress.

9

"I APPRECIATE you bringing these by." Tammy closed
the door behind Olivia, who carried a stack of books.

"Never fear, if you need information the library's
the place to go," Olivia quipped. Olivia's jokes often
came out sort of weird, but Tammy obligingly
laughed. "There's a book on dog care in general.
There's another one in there on different breeds and it
has a small section on greyhounds. Then the other
book is on massage and there's actually a short chapter on animal massage."

Tammy took the books from Olivia. "I was booked
solid today, which is unusual for a Tuesday. But I
managed to run home at lunch and right after work to
check on her. Thanks again for bringing these by."

"Anytime. I still can't believe you have a dog."

"I don't have a dog." Not technically anyway, she
kept reassuring herself.

Olivia cocked an eyebrow. "There's a dog in this
house, isn't there?"

"I'm fostering her. For a month or less. She's not
mine." She'd been handed the chance to help without
risking her heart. She was a professional rendering a

professional service. The client just happened to be a dog.

"Okay. If you say so." Olivia's smirk suggested otherwise. "Where is she? What's her name?"

"Her name is Fair Game and her crate is over there." She pointed to the metal crate snugged in the corner behind the purple armchair and beside the fireplace. Tammy didn't add that the dog seemed to enjoy the Christmas tree lights and that Tammy had surmised this because the dog possessed an incredibly expressive face. Olivia would read all kinds of nonsense into that observation.

"What kind of name is Fair Game?" Olivia wrinkled her nose.

"It was her racing name."

"Well, she needs a proper dog name like Duchess or Trixie."

Ugh. Like anyone would call such a regal animal Trixie. "That'll be up to whoever adopts her." Tammy opened the crate door. "Here, I'll let her out so you can meet her properly."

Thus far, the dog had proven herself incredibly well behaved. Tammy could see how some people might get used to coming home to a pet. Some people, but not her. She didn't need that heartache all over again.

The dog walked out of the crate and stood patiently at Tammy's side, as if she belonged there. Instinctively, Tammy ran her hand down the dog's neck.

"Hello, Fair Game. I'm your aunt Olivia," Olivia crooned, leaning down to stroke the dog's neck. "Oh, you poor baby." Olivia looked up at Tammy. "She's a bag of bones."

The dog was extremely thin, but then again, she was supposed to be. Of course, Olivia was used to Hortense. That cat was so fat Olivia couldn't find a rib if she had to.

"She weighs sixty pounds, but Niall, I mean Dr. Fortson, says she's tall for a female and should weigh closer to seventy. Weight gain is one of the things we're working on in the next month."

"We?"

"Trena followed Niall and Fair Game over last night. The three of us worked up a list of therapy objectives. Weight gain plays into it." Tammy had never been part of a team or joint effort before. It had felt a little odd at first, but she'd actually enjoyed listening to Niall and Trena cover the medical aspect and being asked her opinion from a massage standpoint.

The dog stood beside Tammy and regarded Olivia.

"That's awesome. She'll be beautiful when she fills in a little bit." Olivia looked at the dog who stood solemnly between them. "Is she always so excited?"

First the dog was too skinny and now she wasn't energetic enough. What was wrong with Olivia today? "She's not a jump-around, in-your-face kind of dog."

"I see." Olivia looked at her with a mixture of surprise and conjecture. Tammy realized she'd sounded a bit defensive. "She seems very attached to you."

Tammy shifted from one foot to the other and patted the dog's neck. The dog seemed to like her for no good reason. "She's comfortable with me. Why don't you sit down? You must be tired."

Olivia sat. "I'm not just tired, I'm beat. And the fire's nice."

"Didn't you say Luke's out of town? Eat dinner with me."

"I'm tempted. I've developed a monstrous appetite. At this rate, I'll be a blimp by the time the baby comes. But I need to feed Hortense."

Tammy eyed her oh-so-thin sister who didn't carry an ounce of spare flesh. "I don't think you're capable of blimping. And that cat could live off of her own fat for a week. Eating two hours later certainly won't hurt her. It's tuna casserole." Tammy knew Olivia would stay now.

"Ooooh. My favorite comfort food." Once their mother left, it had become Tammy's specialty. Olivia sank back onto the couch cushions with a grin. "Okay. Twist my arm. Hortense will survive and it feels wonderful just to sit."

"Then sit while I put together the salad and heat up the bread."

"I should help." Olivia started to stand.

Tammy waved her back onto the couch. "No. You sit, like a good sister."

"But I feel useless."

"Okay. You can watch the dog and make sure she doesn't do anything she shouldn't."

"Oh, yeah." Olivia raised her brows at the quiet animal. "She looks like she's into everything."

"Then your job should be easy."

Tammy started out of the room and the dog followed. She turned around. "Stay."

And the dog stayed until Tammy started walking again and then she followed. "Stay."

Olivia smirked from her vantage point on the sofa. Tammy tried leaving the dog behind three more times and three more times the dog followed. Finally, she threw both beast and sister an exasperated look. "Fine. You come with me and you just sit there." She shook a warning finger at Olivia. "And don't say anything."

"My lips are zipped," Olivia said, her eyes alight with laughter.

"That would be best."

Fair Game's nails clicked along the hardwood floors behind Tammy as they walked into the kitchen. In the kitchen's confines, Tammy turned to the dog but couldn't muster any real irritation. "You don't need to get used to me and you don't need to get used to being here."

"Did you say something to me?" Olivia called from the den, amusement evident in her tone.

"No. I was...uh, talking to myself." Tammy turned on the oven and looked at the dog. This time she whispered, "See, now she's laughing at me because I'm talking to you. I can't even believe I'm talking to you."

Fair Game responded by settling into a sitting position, her long legs tucked beneath her, looking more like an overgrown hare than a dog.

Tammy had half a cucumber left to slice when the doorbell rang. Olivia called out, "I'll get it."

A shiver slid over her as she recognized Niall's voice. She dropped the cucumber and snatched up a dish towel. The last thing she wanted was her sister, the hormonal matchmaker, and Niall spending time together.

By the time she made it out of the kitchen, Fair Game on her heels, Niall was inside and the front door was closed. It was ridiculous the way her heart flip-flopped and her belly fluttered when he smiled as if simply seeing her made his day. "Hi."

"Hi. I just met your sister. I didn't want to interrupt but I thought I should check on the patient after I took care of my brood."

Niall squatted down to the dog's level. "How are you, girl?"

"Niall has two cats and two dogs," Tammy explained to Olivia. She refrained from pointing out that he looked awesome in moss green shirt.

He ran his hands along the dog's hindquarters. "How's her limp?" he asked, looking up at her from his squatting position. He had the most extraordinary eyes. And he'd asked her a question.

She pulled herself together. "Marginal improvement this morning and quite a bit tonight."

"Why don't you stay for dinner, Niall? Tammy always makes a huge tuna casserole. I'm sure you're hungry. And Tammy's a wonderful cook."

Heat crawled up her face, and not the I-can't-wait-to-jump-your-bones variety. Oh. My. God. She was already sleeping with the man and she was still embarrassed by Olivia's obvious matchmaking attempts. What was next? Having Tammy open her mouth so he could check out her teeth? Or maybe Olivia could point out how Tammy's wide hips would be great for childbearing? Hormones or not, Olivia was out of control.

And about the only thing Tammy could do was second the invitation. "We'd love to have you join us."

"Are you sure it wouldn't be any trouble?" Niall looked hungry and eager. He looked that way a lot. It was sort of endearing.

"Not at all," she assured him.

"Great. Excuse me, I'll be right back." Olivia headed to the bathroom. Apparently another benefit of pregnancy—a bladder the size of a walnut.

The door had barely closed before Niall pulled her into his arms and kissed her like a starving man. He came up for air and leaned his forehead against hers.

"Every time I passed my office today, all I could think about was last night. Sitting at my desk today was torture."

The look in his dark eyes clearly said he was ready to take up where they'd left off the night before. And, God help her, she wanted his hands and mouth all over her again. "Niall, you can't look at me like that. At least, not until my sister leaves."

"Like what?"

"Like that. Like you can't wait to—"

"I can't," he interrupted, nuzzling her neck.

"You don't even know what I was going to say." And she was fast forgetting as he nibbled at the sensitive spot just below her ear.

"Whatever it was, I want to." His hands skimmed beneath her sweater and stroked the length of her back while his lips explored her neck. She ought to pull back. She really should. She would in just a minute, but he felt so good.

Finally she mustered the wherewithal to step out of his arms. "Stop. Remember, we're going to be discreet."

His hand molded her breast through her sweater, in a gesture that screamed possessiveness. "I don't care who knows."

His thumb teased against her nipple and she leaned into him, even as she argued with him. "Good for you. I care. Especially not Olivia."

"Why especially not Olivia?"

"She's not herself right now. She's pregnant—you know, very emotional."

"But what's that got to do with—"

The toilet flushed and Tammy smacked his hand away. She straightened her clothes and he reluctantly shoved his hands in his pockets.

"Just behave. And don't look at me like that." Well, that was a change. *Her* admonishing someone to behave.

"I'll try. But I probably need one more kiss to sustain me through dinner." His mouth swooped down on hers and he crushed her to him. It was fast and hard and left her totally hot. He released her and she took a step back, almost tripping over the dog. Fair Game's presence offered a much safer subject than her sister's desire to marry her off.

"Did Trena find out anything else about Fair Game today?" Tammy managed a normal, although slightly breathless, voice.

Olivia rejoined them, looking at the two of them. Her sharp-eyed sister didn't miss Tammy's flushed face.

"Niall was just bringing me up to date on the dog," Tammy said.

Olivia nodded. "Please, don't let me interrupt."

"The owners we found through the National Association—their number was disconnected and they've moved from that address. It's a dead end," Niall said. "So, the better shape we can get her in, the faster we can find a new home for her."

"I'd say she's responding well. Much less nervous. More confident. She's very easy to work with. The cold pack on her leg didn't seem to faze her at all." Tammy kept her tone detached. Fair Game was just another case.

"Perfect. That'll make it much easier to find her a new home—if she makes it."

She knew he wasn't being cruel, just realistic, but his words cut with a surgeon's precision.

"A month, right?"

"Pretty much."

"Good. Thirty days isn't that long." She could last thirty days. She'd managed three years with Earl without any real lasting attachment.

Olivia quizzed Niall on the adoption process and the three of them wandered out to the kitchen. Tammy finished making the salad and then, throughout dinner, conversation flowed easily with lots of laughter sprinkled in.

And always the underlying awareness, the ever-present hunger that simmered between Tammy and Niall. His hand brushed hers when he passed her the rolls and sent shivers down her spine. Her leg bumped his beneath the table and heat flashed through her. A glimpse of passion in his eyes hitched her breath.

Inevitably, the discussion rolled around to Christmas.

"Are you staying in town for Christmas or will you travel to be with your family?" Olivia asked Niall.

A huge grin spread over his face, his enthusiasm giving him an almost boyish look. "I may be a new transplant, but Colthersville is home now. We'll be here. Plus, I'm working Christmas Eve morning. Animals don't seem to realize it's a holiday."

Tammy didn't know she'd been holding her breath until she released it. And it really had nothing to do with her whether he was here or not for the holiday.

She caught the look on Olivia's face and knew what was coming next. Part of her wanted to kick Olivia under the table, the other part of her wanted...what?

"Would you like to join us for Christmas dinner at my house? That is, if you don't have any other plans? Or if you'd prefer your own company, we won't be offended," Olivia offered her most gracious smile.

Niall had told Tammy he didn't like to eat alone and she also had the distinct impression he'd never turn down the offer of food.

"I wouldn't want to intrude on your family," he said without a whole lot of conviction.

"We'd love to have you. I wouldn't have invited you otherwise. Tammy'll swing by and pick Pops up on the way out. Our brother, Marty, and his wife, Darlene, may or may not be there." Olivia laughed. "Not too big of a crowd. There's plenty of room for you. And you would like my husband, Luke."

It was the barest glance, but Niall looked at Tammy, as if he was trying to decide if she wanted him there. "That's awfully nice. I'd love to."

"Good. You could ride out with Tammy and Pops or I can give you directions when the time's closer."

Tammy checked the urge to open her mouth and show her teeth. Red alerts went off in her head. It sounded like couples. It sounded like a setup. Luke and Olivia. Darlene and Marty. Tammy and Niall.

Whoa. She was blowing this out of proportion. By Christmas, she and Niall wouldn't be lovers, simply neighbors. No big deal.

"We can figure it out later." Niall said.

Tammy started until she realized he meant the transportation, not the relationship.

Olivia tried, but couldn't hide a yawn behind her hand. "Sorry. I'm just exhausted these days."

And she still had a twenty-minute drive ahead of her. Tammy pushed her chair back. "Okay, Olivia, I'm officially kicking you out. Time for you to go home and get to bed."

"But the dishes—"

"Are no problem," Tammy said.

"Don't worry about it. I'll help with the dishes," Niall assured Olivia. "It'll take no time."

Olivia stood and swayed on her feet, clearly exhausted. "Okay, maybe I will just go. And poor Hortense is probably starving." *Fat chance.* Olivia'd told Niall all about Hortense during dinner. "It was nice to meet you. If I don't see you before then, I look forward to seeing you at Christmas."

"Likewise. I'm sure I'll be seeing more of you." Niall looked at Tammy. "Why don't I take the dog out back for you before I go?"

Without waiting for a response he grabbed the leash from beside the back door and led the dog out. Tammy walked Olivia to the front door. She didn't like Olivia driving when she was so tired.

"Be careful driving home. And thanks for dropping off the books. I'm glad you stayed for dinner."

"I'm glad I got to meet Niall. He's perfect for you."

"You're delusional."

"Maybe. But I'm neither stupid nor blind. There's so much electricity between the two of you, I almost got zapped a couple of times. Now I'm going to be a good sister and leave so you two can tear one another's clothes off like you've been wanting to do since he showed up tonight."

So much for discretion.

NIALL STARED at the ceiling of Tammy's bedroom, totally spent. Totally content to lie there with her still on top of him, her head resting on his chest, her naked breasts pressed against him.

He lazily swept his hand down her bare back and up again. He didn't think he'd ever tire of the feel of her skin. A dangerous sentiment for a man in a temporary affair.

"Umm." Her sigh stirred his chest hair.

"I liked your sister." He dropped a kiss on her tousled hair.

"Olivia's easy to like. But don't feel like you have to take her up on her Christmas dinner."

"Why wouldn't I want to go? It's free food and very good company."

"I have a feeling the food's the main attraction." She laughed and propped her chin on her crossed hands. She idly skimmed her toe along his calf. "You'll like their place. It's great. The house sits in the middle of two hundred acres, some of it in open field but most of it wooded. Memphis and Gigi would love it."

"If it's fenced, you should take Fair Game out next week to let her run. The exercise would be good for her."

"What if it's too much for her?"

He rimmed the dimple above her right butt cheek with his finger. Tammy had an awesome set of dimples. "Wait until you see her run. It's what she was bred to do. But I could always come with you if you're worried about her injuring herself."

"Why don't we play it by ear?" She reached up and traced the scar on his upper lip with her thumb. "How did that happen?"

"Does it bother you?" He'd always been self-conscious about his scar.

"Only from the standpoint that it's terribly sexy."

"Do you really think so?"

"Definitely. Hasn't a woman ever told you that before?"

"No."

"Then there's something wrong with the women you've known. You've got this gorgeous mouth and then this mysterious scar. It keeps you from being perfect and adds an element of mystery."

She thought he was close to perfect? And mysterious? And she'd called his mouth gorgeous.

"You are very, very good for my ego." She was good for him period. When he was with her, he felt more alive than he ever had in his life.

"So, where'd you get that scar?" She shifted and her nipples teased against his chest.

"It's not very glamorous. Certainly not very sexy." He grimaced. "I don't want to spoil the image you have of me."

She played her finger along the line. "Now I definitely have to know."

"I fell and busted my lip on the toilet when I was a kid." He laughed at the dismal truth.

Tammy laughed with him, not at him. "You're right. It's not very glamorous. But it's still very sexy. How old were you?" She lazily stroked his collarbone, as if she, too, needed to touch him, even though they were still in full body contact.

"The day before my fifth birthday. I had a heck of a time eating birthday cake with the stitches in my lip. It also made for some interesting birthday pictures—I'll show you one day. I had one fat lip for a couple of days. Mom still laughs about it."

She grew very still, her hand motionless over his heart. "Are you close to your parents?"

Something in her tone and her very stillness told Niall there was more to this question than met the eye. "I suppose. They divorced when I was a sophomore in college. My sister, Lydia, had just graduated from high school and she took it pretty hard. My older brother, Bart, and I were both into our own thing. It was a little weird going home for holidays for a while, but we've all adjusted. They've both remarried and seem happy enough."

"They stayed together for you kids?" she asked.

He stroked her hair, enjoying the silky play against his fingers. "It sort of looks that way. Except I really don't remember them not getting along. Mom says they just sort of drifted apart."

"And you still want to get married?"

He wasn't a man to take chances, but he stood on the edge of the cliff and jumped. "Are you proposing?" A quirky feeling settled in his belly, despite his teasing tone.

He felt her harsh intake of breath. "That's not funny, Niall."

He'd never heard such a sharp tone from her before. What had he expected? That she'd profess he was just the man she'd been waiting for? Yeah, right. "No, I don't suppose it is funny. My parents were happy together for several years. They had three good kids. They're happy enough now, even if it's not with each other. Sure, I still want to get married. I want to wake up in the morning and see my wife's head on the pillow next to mine. I want to know she'll be there when I come home at night." Funny how her face was etched on both those pictures in his mind.

"You're such a romantic."

He was pretty damn sure she didn't mean that as a compliment this time. And he was pretty sure this wasn't about marriage but more about their parents.

"How old were you when your mother left?"

"Nine." Even though she remained atop him, she withdrew as obviously as if she'd walked to the other side of the room.

"That must've been tough, being bounced from parent to parent."

"There wasn't any bouncing going on. She just left. We came home from school one day and she was gone. She packed her clothes, left a note propped on the kitchen counter and that was that." Her voice, usually so rich with emotion, lacked any inflection.

Damn. He'd misunderstood. He thought her parents had divorced and she'd been shuffled between parents—not totally abandoned by her mother.

"You never heard from her? Not a phone call or a postcard or a birthday card?" Niall recalled the times his mom had hauled him to Little League, brought cupcakes into school on his birthday and sat by his bed when he'd had a nightmare, and his heart ached for Tammy.

"I don't even know if she's still alive." Tension underscored her matter-of-fact words.

"Have you ever tried to find her?"

"Why would I want to do that?"

"To lay it to rest."

"I don't need to see her. I came to terms with her leaving years ago." Despite the hard set of her jaw, he saw that she meant it. "What would really bother me, what I don't want, is your pity."

"It's a good thing. You wouldn't get it. Do you really think I could ever see you as an object of pity?" She gave him an inscrutable look. "It just shows what a strong person you are."

He wrapped his arms around her and rolled them both to their sides. "Now I can see you better." With a finger beneath her chin, he tilted her head up to meet his gaze. "You're a lot of things. Pitiful isn't one of them. You're funny, refreshing, sensual, generous and brave. Oh, and there is that beautiful thing." He wasn't just being flippant. It wasn't nearly as important as the other things that made her who she was.

"You make me sound like a veritable paragon of virtue. How do you suppose my three husbands were able to walk away?"

That was a question that begged answering. Why would a man walk away from her? Not once, not twice, but three times. He'd actually spent some time thinking about it and only had one plausible explanation.

"It's simple. Idiots. They were idiots."

He coaxed a glimmer of a smile from her. A nasty thought occurred to him. "Do you think I'm a loser because Mia didn't want to marry me?"

"Clearly she was an idiot as well." And clearly she was responding tongue-in-cheek.

"I'm sort of serious." As in he needed some serious reassurance.

"No. I think you and Mia started out together and wound up on different paths. From what I can tell, *you're* the veritable paragon of virtue."

"I'm trying to decide if I should risk letting you see my bad side."

She boldly appraised him, cocking her head to take in a different angle. "All your sides look pretty good to me. And it doesn't matter how nice you are, you can't stay the night."

He was beginning to understand her, to read between her lines. Things had gotten too personal, too serious between them. Like an engineer controlling a train, she'd switched tracks, steering them back to her comfort zone. He followed her lead. "Are you kicking me out? The night's still young."

She skimmed her hand over his equipment, which found a new lease on life. She leaned down and teased her tongue along his thickening length. "If you try hard, you might convince me to let you stay a little longer."

He was sure of three things. He'd agreed to an affair that would end far too soon. He was perilously close to falling in love with her, if he hadn't already. And the third thing he knew for sure, the only one he had any real control over, was that she wanted him as much as he wanted her, for the moment, at least.

Niall settled against the pillows, his body tensing with anticipation. "I feel sure I'm up to that task."

10

TAMMY WATCHED Niall sleep, his dark head a contrast to the pillow case, his size dwarfing her double bed. One day left. Twenty-four hours from now this would be over.

She memorized the play of light and shadows across his face, the feel of his muscular thigh beneath her leg, the even rhythm of his breathing, the slight arch to his left brow, that sexy scar, his smell on her sheets and her body.

Niall was so...Niall. With her usual aplomb for screwing up a relationship, she'd picked the wrong man to scratch an itch. Niall was too much man for such a little slot.

When she was with him she didn't feel alone, it was as if he saw into her heart and her head. In two short weeks he'd woven himself into the fabric of her life— impromptu picnics, late-night stargazing, jokes he brought home from the office, progress meetings with him and Trena, watching the dog run for the first time, and long nights of making love—leaving her life richer, fuller. And that frightened her beyond all reason.

She should've taken Lowell, in every sense of the

word, when she had the opportunity. Lowell wouldn't have made love to her in a way that was both exciting and achingly tender. Lowell would've never asked about her mother. Lowell wouldn't have foisted a dog on her. Lowell wouldn't have charmed her sister over dinner, while eyeing Tammy as if she were a piece of precious china.

Fate had a wicked sense of timing. Where had Niall been ten years ago when she'd still believed she had a chance at happy ever after?

She could never be what Niall needed and she wouldn't let him settle for less. Come hell or high water, her heart would remain her own and she'd stick to her end of the bargain.

NIALL RESTED his head along the back of Tammy's sofa. Tonight was their last night, the self-appointed end to their "fling." He'd definitely been thinking with the wrong head when he'd agreed to those terms.

"Do you want a beer?" Tammy asked from the kitchen doorway.

"Sure." He started to stand. "But I can get it."

"Don't be silly. You're a guest." Niall felt a bit as if she'd just put him in his place. He'd increasingly had a sense of her keeping him at arm's distance. Like an emotional advance and retreat, when he got too close, she retreated. If she'd always run from her emotions this way, and he'd bet she had, it was no small wonder her first three marriages had failed. Niall pushed aside his desperate sense of time running out.

Fair Game wandered over and planted her chin on his knee. "Hi, girl. How're you doing?"

Damn if this didn't feel like home. Him, the dog, Tammy. He just needed Memphis, Gigi, Tex and Lolita to complete the picture.

Tammy walked in with two beers. "She wants you to rub her chest. She likes the area just beyond her two front legs."

Niall took the beer with his left hand and, with his right, rubbed the area Tammy had pinpointed. The dog closed her eyes and leaned against his leg.

"I told you she liked it." Tammy sat down next to Niall, one foot tucked beneath her.

"Yeah. She seems pretty happy. We should introduce her to my crew and see how they get along."

Something curiously akin to longing flickered across her face. "I know it's early, but have you had any luck finding her a home?"

"Trena hasn't mentioned it." Which would be because he'd instructed Trena to hold off, sure that given enough time, Tammy wouldn't want to give up the dog. Just as he was hoping she wouldn't want to give up the man.

"I just thought with Christmas only a week away some nice family might adopt her. She'd make someone a great Christmas present."

Yeah, and Niall was looking right at that *someone* if that someone would acknowledge it. "Actually, the chances of her finding a home before Christmas are pretty slim. People want puppies and kittens at

Christmas." Fair Game bumped Tammy's knee with her needle nose and rubbed her head against Tammy's leg with obvious affection. "It looks to me as if she's found herself a pretty good home."

As if to give credence to his declaration, the dog stepped up on the couch, pretty as you please, curled up next to Tammy like an overgrown canine cat, and placed her head in Tammy's lap. The look on Tammy's face as she swung her gaze to the dog was absolutely priceless. She looked cute with her mouth hanging open.

Niall laughed—he seemed to do a lot of that when he was with her. "There you go. Your own personal sixty-five-pound lapdog."

Tammy definitely looked flustered. "She's never done this before."

"Want me to get her down?"

Tammy looked at Fair Game. The dog looked back with obvious adoration. "No. Just leave her. Unless you think the next people who get her will have a problem with her getting on the furniture."

She did the same thing with the dog that she did with him. The dog got too close and Tammy brought up the dog's leaving.

"You know, she doesn't have to go anywhere else."

"I told you from the beginning, I'm not an animal person." Did she realize the entire time she was disavowing her affinity for this dog and animals in general, she was scratching Fair Game behind one ear?

"And I told you I think you're wrong." She was

scared to open herself up to loving an animal again, but that didn't have jack to do with some bogus affinity.

She slid her hand onto his thigh, her touch branding him through his khaki pants. Her eyes took on a smoky look he'd come to recognize. Good things came to both of them when she had that look. Her fingers slid closer to his crotch. "Are we going to spend our last night arguing? Is that what you really want to do?" she asked.

He knew exactly what was going on; he'd come to recognize the pattern. They headed into emotional areas and she pulled them back to the physical. And he'd expected the edge to wear off the physical. It was just the opposite. Things just got hotter between them. Niall closed his eyes. Jesus, he was hard already. She stroked him through his khakis and he shuddered.

No, he didn't want to argue. This was the last night to play out their fantasies. He opened his eyes and reached for her. Niall slid her dress off her shoulder. "Do you know what I really want?" He teased his fingertips against her shoulder.

"Tell me."

Niall grabbed his courage and threw out a fantasy he'd had ever since she'd mentioned dancing. "I'd like for you to dance for me. Do you think you could do that for me?"

"I'm not well versed in ballet," she flirted.

"That's good. I didn't have ballet moves in mind."

"You don't strike me as a strip club kind of guy."

"I'm not." His buddies had dragged him along to see exotic dancers once during a friend's bachelor party. That'd been more than enough. "But I've had this fantasy going ever since you mentioned dancing the other day."

Oh, yeah, she liked that idea. A decidedly naughty smile curled her lips. "Any requests?"

"Your choice." His temperature had already risen a couple of degrees just talking about it.

"I know just the thing. But you've got to put Bella in the kitchen."

"Bella?"

She shifted on her end of the couch. "Uh, the dog."

"So, you call her Bella?" Yeah, and she wanted to find the dog another home.

"Not really. Well, yeah, I guess I do. She doesn't answer to Fair Game. Anyway, that's a lame name for any animal. And it's just that she's beautiful…" Niall lost his battle with laughter. She leveled an evil look his way which he knew she didn't really mean. "Never mind, just put the dog in the kitchen."

Niall hoisted himself up off the couch. "Come on girl."

"You'll need to take her bed," Tammy said.

Niall raised his brows in inquiry.

"The floor's hard and she doesn't have a lot of padding. I don't want her undoing all of my massage. There's a box of dog treats on the counter if you'll give her one for going with you."

"Right." Niall tugged the bed out of the crate.

Tammy could deny it all she wanted, but she was smitten with this sweet little dog. "Come on, Bella."

Bella followed obediently to the kitchen. Niall settled her in, giving her the dog biscuit as Tammy had instructed. He returned to the den.

Tammy had turned out the lights and lit candles along the mantel. Gas logs burned in the fireplace and the Christmas tree lights twinkled. She stood in front of the fireplace, backlit by the licking flames of the gas logs and candles.

Niall sat on the sofa. Tension hung thick in the air, mingling with the exotic incense curling from the burner, and his pulse quickened. She hadn't started and he was already hard and throbbing.

With one click of a remote, a sultry, sexy beat started. He wasn't sure who sang it, but he recognized the lyrics—hot, suggestive lyrics that proposed they "get it on."

He was ready. She did some wiggly, shimmy move with her hips. Make that more than ready. She pulled her dress over her head and flung it somewhere past his head and he reminded himself to breathe as she moved to the music in a matching black bra and panties and boots. She turned her back to him and did some quick move, bending at the waist. She shot him a wicked smile through her legs and jiggled her behind.

"Oh, baby."

She pivoted, straightened back up, and she danced over to him. With a provocative glance she put one foot on the sofa cushion next to him and climbed up over his lap, bracing the other foot on the arm of the furniture.

Oh, yeah. She wound down low, her panty-clad mound mere inches from his mouth, her luscious thighs tantalizingly close, the heady musk of her arousal surrounding him. She leaned forward and unhooked her bra, freeing her breasts. He leaned back for a better view. She shimmied her shoulders and her magnificent chest performed its own dance.

Lust and absolute excitement fogged his brain and hardened him to an almost unbearable degree. Part of him wanted to touch her, taste her. The other part of him didn't want anything this erotic to end. She stepped down off the couch and the heel of her boot caught on the sofa cushion. Niall caught her as she fell back. With a laugh and a sassy smile, she regained her footing and danced away. It could've ruined a very sexy performance. Instead, it made it even hotter, more arousing because this was real. Her and him.

The song ended. "Did you like that?" Her throaty question feathered along his nerve endings.

Obviously, no one died from a hard-on; otherwise, he'd be a dead man.

"Come here." Was that low, thick voice really his own?

"No." She shook her head, and her breasts jiggled in a motion that damn near unhinged him. A wicked, teasing glint lit her eyes. "I'm going to start this song again and you're going to dance for me."

She'd picked a hell of a time to joke around. "Yeah, right. Now, come here."

She planted her hands on her hips, sending her breasts into another dance all their own. She. Was. Killing. Him. "I'm not kidding. You've heard of dancing for your supper...." Her blue eyes sparkled. "Well, you've got to dance for something else."

If she'd asked him to do anything else... "I'd really like to do this for you, but I can't dance."

"Niall, I almost busted my butt dancing. Was that a problem for you?"

"No, but—"

Tammy sank into the armchair next to the sofa, draping one boot-clad leg over the chair's arm, the other foot on the floor, her legs splayed, the entrance to her own private paradise barely covered by a strip of black satin panties. Her navel ring glinted in the firelight. "I'm sure you can dance. I think you've just never been properly motivated." She cupped her breasts, fingering her plum-hued nipples. They puckered into tight points of invitation. His erection strained against his briefs and his mouth ran dry.

She slid her hands down her body, a slow sensuous caress, over her stomach and hips. With her palms against her inner thighs, she spread her legs. Even from the sofa, he could see the black satin of her panties was darker between her legs. Wet. Whether he could or it was just his imagination, he smelled her musky scent. She ran her tongue over the fullness of her lips, as if she were anticipating a treat. She slipped a finger beneath the edge of her panties and she breathed a little harder and faster. Or was that him? She edged her finger out of her panties, brought it to her breast and rubbed it over her nipple.

His groan echoed off the walls. Damn it to hell. She wasn't fighting fair.

"There's motivation, and then there's motivation." Niall stood. "Just remember, you asked for this."

With a soft laugh and a hot look, Tammy hit the remote and started the music. Dancing was a challenge on a good day, how the hell was he supposed to do this with a hard-on? He comforted himself with the thought that she'd at least have sex with him for trying. Niall began to move in time to the music—or at least he hoped it was in time to the music.

It was amazing how the glint of admiration in Tammy's eyes encouraged him and helped him forget he'd never owned a sense of rhythm, bad or otherwise. Swaying in time to the music and slowly taking his shirt off was easier than he'd thought. His shirt joined Tammy's clothes piled in the floor. By the time he worked his belt free and slid it through the loops, he was really getting into it, not feeling a bit ridiculous, as he'd thought he might.

He'd always just been Niall. Easygoing, laid-back, rock-steady Niall. Now, for the first time in his life, he was sexy, wicked Niall. And he liked it. By the time the song ended he had the hip thrust down pat and had worked his way down to his briefs.

Judging by her lustful smile, Tammy enjoyed his show. "I thought you couldn't dance."

"I can't."

"I beg to differ."

Another sultry, hip-grinding tune started. Now that he was getting the hang of this dancing thing, he sort of liked it. Niall held out his hand. "Come dance with me."

"I've created a monster."

"I never had the right dance partner before."

Slowly Tammy rose to her feet and placed her hands in his. Both seminaked, they swayed to the rhythm of the music, close but only touching with their hands. It was terribly arousing for their bare skin to be so close.

Her breasts glanced against his chest like a feather gusseted by the wind. The brief contact sizzled through him, straight to his groin.

"You are a beautiful man." Her husky assertion stirred against his chest. When he was with her, he felt like more than he'd ever felt before. Like he was a superhero. Like he could accomplish anything.

Tammy leaned forward and dragged her tongue across his flat male nipple. Fire arced through him. Her marauding tongue flicked against his other nipple. He dropped his head back and gave himself over to the pure pleasure of the moment. She licked at the base of his neck at the same moment her panty-clad mound ground against his arousal.

A man could only stand so much. Niall dropped to the couch, pulling her down astride him. ''Dancing lessons are over.''

TAMMY LAY VERY STILL. Very quiet. Waiting for her equilibrium, her sense of self to return. Nothing in her thirty-two years had prepared her for *that*. For *this*. For the connection she felt with Niall. The sense of change. The sense she'd never be the same again.

Sex wasn't supposed to be this soul-shattering experience that mined emotions. She'd had plenty of orgasms, but they'd all been her own. But this time, Niall had been there with her. Not in just the physical sense, that wasn't a novelty. It was an emotional and mental union, as if she'd united with a soul mate.

Slowly her sense of self returned, cloaking her in the detachment she'd lost in the heat of their passion. From the kitchen, a mournful sound arose. Tammy jacknifed up, almost whacking Niall's chin with her head. ''What's the matter? It sounds like she's dying. You've got to do something, Niall.''

Niall pulled her back down to his shoulder. ''She'll be okay. She's just rooing. It's a greyhound thing. She'll quit in a minute.''

The awful sound continued, sending apprehension down her spine, despite his reassurance. ''But why's she doing that?''

''Separation anxiety,'' he said.

Tammy totally related. She knew, soul deep, that her fling was over with Niall. On the brink of suffering her own brand of separation anxiety, she felt a bit like rooing right along with Bella.

"She'll be okay," he added.

"How long will it last?" She couldn't bear much more of the dog's mournful cry. It was ripping her apart.

"It's like having a baby crying. You don't want to reinforce her behavior by giving in to it."

"Well, I'm not sure how much longer I can listen to this. She sounds pitiful."

"She's just missing you." There was something about the way he said it, the look in his eye, that made the sentiment his own. Her breath hitched in her throat and her heart flip-flopped.

"You know I'm not an animal lover—"

"You've mentioned that on occasion," he said dryly.

She ignored his interruption, "—but she's really a very sweet dog."

"Yes, Bella seems a very nice girl. A little neurotic…"

That kind of misunderstanding was just the thing that concerned Tammy. What if someone else misunderstood Bella, as well? "She's sensitive, but she most certainly isn't neurotic."

The fire's glow picked up his teasing smirk and the glint in his eye. She laughed and pretended to smack him. She'd never laughed with a man as much as she laughed with Niall. "You jerk. You should feel very guilty about baiting me."

Mercifully, the dog stopped the dreadful sound.

"You're right. I should." He tightened his arm around her. "But I don't."

It had never felt so easy to be with someone. So comfortable. For one crazy moment the idea occurred to her that Niall genuinely liked her for herself—not some image she projected.

With his other hand splayed across her stomach, Niall toyed with her navel ring.

"It's chilly, but not too cold. Let's go outside. Maybe you could put on those flannel pajamas—"

"You like my flannel pajamas?" Just when she thought she had him pegged, he surprised her—like when he danced for her earlier.

"I think you're cute in them." No one had ever accused her of cuteness. She sort of liked it. "Put them on and we can sit outside under your comforter and watch the stars."

He was sexy and tender and quite literally took her breath. "You are the most romantic man I've ever met."

"Do you really think so?"

"Didn't I just say so?"

"Mia always said I was the most pragmatic man she knew."

Mia. Just her name caused the hair on the back of Tammy's neck to stand up. Mia. Shit-for-brains Mia. It was one thing not to want to *marry* Niall—Tammy totally understood and related to that sentiment. But how could Mia not recognize what a great guy she'd had? Shit for brains was the only explanation Tammy could come up with. "It doesn't sound as if you and Mia were suited at all."

"I'm beginning to see, very clearly, that was the case."

"I didn't mean to imply that you and I are suited...."

"There's no implication. We are."

Panic welled inside her. "But I mean, not long-term like, you know."

"Relax. I'm not reading anything into that. I'm not making more of our relationship than there is," he said.

Niall sounded as if he were trying to convince himself as much as her.

11

TAMMY SNUGGLED against Niall's chest, both of the them wrapped in the down-filled comforter.

"I've been kicking around an idea." Niall's deep voice rumbled beneath her cheek. "How long have you had your massage therapy business going?"

"Five months. I'd been going to night school for over a year. When Earl and I separated I moved back in with Pops and went full-time, which finished it up pretty quickly. My brother-in-law called in a favor with his family and helped me get the financial backing for the house and the business, otherwise I probably would've had to work for someone else for a while."

"And has it been slower or faster getting off the ground than you thought?"

"Surprisingly, it's been a little faster than I thought it might. Some days are slow, but for the most part I'm booked. Saturdays are always really busy." Lulled by his warmth and interest in the dark night, she shared her dream. "I'd like to open a day spa. A place where women go to rejuvenate, recharge their batteries. It would offer a variety of massage packages, an esthetician and a nail technician. I've even thought of incorporating some yoga and nutrition classes." She laughed self-consciously. "Not that I've given it any thought or anything."

She sat very still. She'd absolutely die if he laughed at her idea. She hadn't mentioned it to anyone else, not even Olivia. Actually she didn't much care what anyone else thought. Niall's opinion, however, mattered a great deal to her.

"I think that's a great idea."

She sagged with relief that he hadn't jeered at her plans. Not that she'd expected him to, but it would've hurt immeasurably. "Well, I'd definitely need a bigger space than I have now. I've put some numbers together and if the business continues to do as well as it has, I should be ready in five years."

"This actually goes right along with what I've been thinking about. What if I told you I had a way you could pick up extra money?"

It was nice to have a sounding board for her ideas and she was equally interested in his feedback. "I'm listening."

"Bella's responding well to your massage. Of course, it doesn't hurt that she likes you. But Gigi and Memphis like you, too. You don't consider yourself an animal person, but I think you are. Animals are much more discerning than humans and all the animals I've seen you around were quite taken with you."

"Okay." She was intrigued, but not particularly convinced.

"I was thinking...what if we offered animal massage through the veterinary clinic? It would provide an additional benefit to our clients and an additional income source for you."

Excitement sparked inside her. "There could be two levels of massage. A general feel-good massage and a therapeutic massage."

"That's it. We're definitely running on the same wavelength. This could definitely work, especially if you work with horses. As a rule, horse owners are willing to spend lots of money on their animals. What do you think?"

She was darn close to boo-hooing was what she thought. Niall thought enough of her talents that he'd consider her an asset to his practice. "I'm very flattered."

"Don't be." With his arms wrapped around her from behind, he gathered her hands in his. "You have a real talent. That's fact, not flattery."

She entwined her fingers with his. The thought flitted through her mind that Niall's hands represented the whole man, big, strong, capable, yet nurturing and tender.

"I'm flattered just the same. I'd have to think it over some though." Of course, it was also Schill's practice and he'd welcome her with open arms about the time monkeys flew out her butt. She hated to quell Niall's enthusiasm, but she had to address it if he was seriously throwing this out on the table. "What about Dr. Schill? I can't see him wanting to work with me."

His thumb stroked lazy circles against the back of

her hand. "Schill runs a tight ship and he's all about making money."

"Money or no money, if he grabs me again, he's gonna be singing soprano," she said.

"Trust me, he won't get out of line," he promised, his voice hard.

Niall had invested money in this practice. It wasn't as if he could just leave and find another job if things didn't work out here. Guilt gnawed at her. "I should've never brought up the Thanksgiving incident. I don't want to cause trouble between you and Schill."

"Of course you should've told me about that. He was way out of line. But as for work, I don't anticipate any trouble. We'll just all know where we stand."

"When would you want to start?"

"It'd take some time for us to get the word out, but I think it'd catch on quickly. We could start after the holiday. Would you be willing to see cases on your day off at the clinic? Of course, the horses would have to be a house call. Pretty hard to get a horse onto a massage table at your place or the clinic. And the aroma definitely wouldn't add to the atmosphere in either place."

She snickered. She loved—uh, make that, appreciated his sense of humor. "Now that it's too cold to sunbathe, I could spare the time."

He pushed aside her hair and nuzzled the back of her neck, sending shivers cascading down her spine. "Never let anything get in the way of your sunbathing. And I'd appreciate it if you'd let me know the next time you plan to do it."

She playfully smacked him. "Pervert."

He laughed, his warm breath gusting against her sensitive nape. "I prefer opportunist."

She'd expected to take a lover, but never to find a friend. She'd miss snuggling beneath the stars with him. Who was she kidding? She'd miss everything about spending time with him, the conversation, the easy comradery, the hot sexual tension—the whole enchilada. Somehow, somewhere along the line he'd come to mean too much to her.

"I'm going to miss you," he said in a quiet, somber tone. It was as if he'd tuned in and tracked her thoughts.

Tears gathered behind her eyes and she engaged in some serious emotional backtracking. "It's been great sex."

"Phenomenal. And you know it's been more than that. You're fun to be with. I see things in a different light when I'm with you," he said.

His words wrapped around her like another blanket. They meant more than hollow odes to her beauty because they were directed at the inner woman, not the outer trappings. How could she guard her heart against such an assault? *Keep it light.*

"Well, as a founding member of this mutual admiration society, let me say you're not too bad yourself. Sensitive, sexy, romantic, bright, a little warped."

"Don't stop now. You're on a roll and I like it, except for that warped business." His breath was warm against the shell of her ear. "We could always look at extending—"

She touched her fingers to his lips. "No. Don't even say it. This way we end on a good note, while we can still be friends."

"That has to be one of the most odious phrases in the English language." She felt him tense against her back, or was it merely her own tension?

It wasn't fair of him to tempt her. She'd been holding on to this affair ending like a lifeline. "If we continue as lovers, how do you expect to meet your dream woman, the one to travel the matrimonial highway with you?"

"Sarcasm doesn't become you."

Hurt was mixed in with rising anger in his voice. She was glad it was dark on the patio and she didn't have to see his face, watch disillusionment replace all the fondness he'd expressed earlier. One day he'd thank her for this. "Too bad. I'm trying very hard to look out for your best interests. We have phenomenal, earth-shattering sex together and you're fun to be with, but that doesn't change the fact that we have vastly different goals when it comes to our personal lives."

"What if I said I don't want to marry you? What would you say to that?"

"I'd say it's a damn good thing."

"So, are you moving on to Lowell next?"

"What do you know about Lowell?"

"You mentioned him the first night we made love. You said you should be with him instead. So, is Lowell next in line?" Sarcasm wasn't too attractive on Niall, either.

"He could be. We left it that I'm supposed to call him when I'm ready to go out with him," she volleyed back.

"Well, let me know if Lowell needs any tips on what you like."

She knew he was upset, but she wasn't going to sit around and listen to this. This wasn't dialogue that would get them anywhere but into a slinging match.

Tammy stood. "It's time for you to go."

Without another word, Niall got to his feet.

Tammy gathered the comforter and walked to the back door.

"Wait. Tammy—"

She looked back at him silhouetted against the night sky. They both needed some distance before they could have a rational discussion. "You know the way out. Latch the gate behind you."

She closed the door and leaned against it. She buried her face in the comforter and gave way to the tears that had threatened earlier.

Ridiculous, really, that ending a two-week affair hurt tremendously more than ending any of her marriages.

DAMN IT ALL TO HELL. He'd acted like a supremo jerk last night. He'd just been so damn frustrated when

Tammy steadfastly refused to even discuss an ongoing relationship. How had she become so important to him in such a short period of time? God, he could barely stand to think about another man holding her while they watched the night sky, making love to her in front of that fireplace. Just the idea twisted a sharp knife in his gut.

He poured himself a cup of strong, black coffee. Maybe caffeine would help. Sleep would've been even better, but that hadn't happened. He'd lain in bed all night with the previous evening replaying itself like a bad video loop in his head.

"Am I just being obsessive? Possessive? You know I've never been jealous before. What's up with this?" he asked the dogs.

Memphis and Gigi looked up from their respective dishes but didn't offer any useful advice.

"Don't worry about it, guys. I'll be fine. She's actually done me a big favor. Getting over Mia wasn't that hard and we were together for eight years. Tammy and I had a two-week fling. We'll be neighbors and friends and this'll turn out just great."

He put a little spin on the situation for the dogs. He turned up the cup and swallowed a scalding mouthful of the wicked brew. He made the world's worst coffee. "Okay. That's about all I can stand of that. Now I've got to drag myself over there and apologize. And I want this off my conscience today." He opened the back door, turning them out for their post-breakfast pee. "I'll let you guys back in before I leave for work. Wish me luck."

The dogs took off across the deck, heading for open ground without even a backward glance.

He cut across his yard. He rang the doorbell and shoved his hands into his pockets because he didn't know quite what else to do with them. After what felt like an eternity, but was probably only a minute, Tammy opened the door. "Yes?"

"Can I come in? Only for a minute. I've got to be at the office by seven-thirty."

Silently she stepped back, opening the door wider, and allowed him in. Niall had never seen her this way. Her hair stuck up at odd angles all over her head and she didn't have a trace of makeup on. Her lashes, usually heavy with dark mascara, were a sandy brown. "This is the morning after. It's not very pretty."

She looked younger and vulnerable, but still beautiful. "I like the way you look. But that's beside the point. I didn't come over to look at you. I came over to apologize."

He'd seen her retreat emotionally any number of times in the last two weeks. But now, he watched her lay the bricks and surround herself with a wall. "No problem. We all say things at one time or another that we don't mean."

Despite her superficial smile, her eyes were as distant as if he were a stranger seeking directions. God, this was worse than eating dirt. He'd truly screwed up.

"I was way out of line. I hope you'll forgive me."

"I accept your apology. Now don't give it another thought."

Frustrated, Niall clamped down on his impulse to yell at her not to do this. But how did you complain about a woman who was graciously, albeit distantly, accepting your apology and telling you not to worry about it? She'd shut him out to the point that he'd just look like an even bigger jerk-off.

"Thanks for stopping by. I've got to hit the shower and I'm sure you need to get to work." She efficiently, impersonally ushered him out the door and closed it in his face, leaving him standing on the front stoop.

Shit, shit and shit. He thought about kicking the plastic Santa on the front lawn but he hadn't pitched a tantrum since his younger sister had conscripted his G.I. Joe for the most unwarriorlike task of escorting her Barbie to a wedding. It wasn't Santa's fault, he wasn't seven years old and it wasn't likely to endear him to Tammy. All very good reasons for him to walk back home without kicking anything but his own sorry ass.

He opened the back door and whistled for Gigi and Memphis. They trotted past him and down the hall, heading for their bed in the den.

"It was a wash, in case you were interested."

Gigi backtracked to circle around him once, barking.

For once, he was glad he didn't know what she was saying.

12

NIALL DRUMMED his fingers on his desk. He needed advice. He mentally ran through all his guy friends. Like most couples he knew, he and Mia had been together long enough that his friends were also her friends. And calling one of their friends to discuss another woman, even if he and Mia were quits, didn't seem quite the thing to do. No, he needed a woman's insight.

He picked up the phone and dialed a number from memory, breaking out into a smile when a familiar voice answered. "Hey, Lydia. It's Niall." Even if she was his baby sister, she was still a female and the most likely candidate to shed light on the mysterious workings of the female psyche. "How are things in sunny California?"

"It's just another glamorous day in the life of a navy wife. Danny's been on maneuvers for almost a month. Travis the Terrible—" his three-year old nephew was an unholy terror "—just conked out for an hour nap so he can regroup for the second round of battle this afternoon. I'm wrapping Christmas presents and watching mindless television. Top that if you can."

"I've got a situation," he blurted.

"Uh-oh. You've reverted to Dad's military lingo. It must be serious. What's the sit rep?" But instead of waiting for him to deliver a situation report, she plowed on. "Would this be a chick situation? Does this involve Mia? 'Cause I told you when you broke up that I thought you were better off without her."

"I thought women didn't like to be called chicks."

"It's okay if we're the ones doing the calling."

"No wonder I can't keep all this straight. And no, this isn't about Mia. And yes, you made it abundantly clear what you thought of her. Ambiguity has never been a problem for you."

"Thanks, I think. Now what's going on? Tell Lydie all about it." She used her childhood nickname.

Niall spilled the whole story. Well, almost the whole story. He didn't see any point in bringing out the particulars of their sexcapades.

"Whew. That's quite a story." For once, Lydia was serious. "I don't think this is what you want to hear, but if she's offering you the chance to just walk away, that might be the best thing, Niall." She was right. That wasn't what he wanted to hear. "This isn't like when we were kids and moved from place to place. You've made a commitment to be there and this woman sounds like trouble. Why didn't things work out with those three husbands?"

"We've talked a little about it, but it isn't that important. Just like my past with Mia isn't that important now."

"I still think you should walk away."

"There's something special about her."

She huffed, just like their mother did when she was exasperated. "Niall, I can name five of my friends who are special but they haven't been married three times and sworn off commitment. They're young, beautiful and looking for a man to say 'I do.' They'd wrestle naked in a Jell-O pit to get their hands on a nice guy like you."

His sister always made him smile. "Aside from the naked Jell-O wrestling, I've met a couple of women like that here, too."

Lydia sighed heavily on the other end of the phone line. "And let me guess—you're not interested?"

"Not even a little bit." That probably sent her into a fit of eye-rolling.

"Oh, God. This is bad, isn't it?"

"It's looking pretty damn dismal from where I stand."

"You sound seriously bad. Come on, shake it off. You've known her—what? Less than a month?"

"I know it sounds crazy."

"Yeah, it does." He'd have felt better if she hadn't agreed with him so readily. "Niall, this is so unlike you. You're the least impulsive man I know. Don't take this the wrong way, but you verge on boring."

How the hell else was he supposed to take that but as insulting? He opened his mouth, one breath away from telling her he'd recently prepared dinner in the buff and performed a striptease, but a guy had to draw the line at what he confessed to his bratty sister.

Better that she think him a bore than have that kind of ammunition on him.

"I'm not the same man I was before. I've never met anyone like her before."

"Apparently," she said.

Niall was doing a terrible job describing Tammy and his feelings for her. "She's like that layered Mexican bean dip Mom makes."

"What? She gives you gas?"

Point of proof. Once a brat, always a brat.

"No. You look at the top and you see this tempting layer of grated cheese. It looks good. You want it. Your appetite is whetted. But then you find out it's got even better stuff below the cheese."

"Niall."

"What?"

"I'll help you, but you've got to promise me one thing."

"Anything."

"Stick to being a vet and never try your hand at poetry. I don't think she'd be flattered to know she reminds you of a layered bean dip."

"She might. She thinks I'm romantic."

"Then she is seriously weird. I've never known you to do a romantic thing in your practical life."

He'd never been moved to until he met Tammy. "She inspires me."

"Humph. You're serious, aren't you?"

"I think so."

"You need to make sure. She's been through a lot already. She doesn't need you messing with her head—"

"I thought you didn't like the sound of her, and now you're defending her."

"I don't want you to get hurt and she sounds like she's just the one who could do it. I've never heard you like this. You were pissed with Mia, but it was different. You're already freaked out over this woman. And I just don't know if you can make it work with her."

Not making it work meant spending the rest of his life like this. "I've got to make it work, Lydie. If I'd never met her, I would've been okay. I'd have schlepped on doing what I was doing, not really knowing what I was missing."

"The sex is that good?"

"Not just the sex. Everything. She brings a depth to my life, to me, I never had before."

"Danny calls me his missing link," she said, longing threaded through her soft tone.

These long months when Danny was at sea had to be tough on his sister. "Will he be home for Christmas?"

"He's supposed to be. Sorry I sidetracked but I miss him something terrible. Now let's get back to you. Does this mean you've finally found something worth fighting for?"

"What is that supposed to mean?"

"It means everything has always come easy for you. You've never really struggled with or for anything.

Friends, vet school, grades, this new practice. Mia said no and you just walked away, even though it meant good riddance. The way I see it, you can walk away again or you can fight for Tammy."

Niall thought about their affair. He thought back to their conversations. Every time something got too intense, too personal, she used sex as a diversionary tactic. And even toward the end, when he realized what she was doing, he'd let her. If she reduced everything to the physical, there was no room for the emotional.

And he'd bet that she'd done the same thing to all the other men in her life. Talk about holding the world at arm's length. Just letting a dog into her life sent her over the edge. And she was great with animals. Animals sensed the true nature of people. She could smoke screen people with her bad reputation shtick, but animals didn't care about reputations.

"Thanks, Lydie."

"But I didn't do anything."

"Sure you did. You listened and things are a little clearer now."

"So, what are you going to do about it?"

"Well, I don't know exactly."

"Hmm, that's what I thought. I take it you haven't told her how you feel about her."

"Not exactly."

"Well, that'd be good place to start, don't you think?"

NIALL SAT on her couch. He'd phoned and asked if he could come by. Though Tammy knew the wise answer was *no,* she longed to see him. She'd thought perhaps they were ready to move on to friendly neighbor status as opposed to disgruntled former lovers. But Niall had been wound really tight since he'd arrived. Of course, that could've been the lack of sex. It could make a person edgy. And she should know.

Niall took a deep breath. "You said no games and I went along with it. You said no pretense and I went along with that. Now I'm going to give it to you straight. I'm not going to pretend that I want to walk away from you. I don't. I'm not going to play some game that I don't care if you move on to another man. I do. And I'm not going to pretend that what we have isn't real and special. It is. And I'm not going to pretend I don't love you. I do."

Whew. She really wasn't ready for that. "You don't know me. We're neighbors. We've been lovers. But you can't possibly know me enough to love me." Because if he knew her well, he couldn't possibly love her.

"I'm not sure if you're ready to know how well I know you. You wear your bad-girl reputation like a suit of armor. You hide the real you behind it, keeping everyone at arm's length so they can't see the woman that lies beneath. That what-you-see-is-what-you-get story is your biggest pretense of all."

"Okay. Then here it is. You think you love me, but when you get to know me, the real me, you won't. If

I'm such a fake, then why are you standing here now, wasting your time with someone like me?"

Niall stood and paced to the fireplace. He turned to face her, his eyes intense. "Because, contrary to your argument, I do know the real you. From the moment I met you I was drawn to you."

"No kidding. I was naked."

"It was more than that and you know it. Tell me I'm wrong about two things. Tell me I'm crazy and we don't have this connection. And tell me you don't love me. Tell me it isn't love I see in your eyes. Tell me it isn't love I feel in your touch."

She walked away from him and looked out the window. She clasped her hands to steady them.

"While we're at it, tell me you don't love Bella, too."

Why didn't he just stop? Why didn't he just go? But he wouldn't, until she gave him what he'd come for. The truth. She whirled around. "Okay. I love you. I love you and I love that crazy dog and I even love those quirky animals of yours. But it doesn't change anything."

"The hell it doesn't change anything." The man had lost his mind, wearing that goofy grin.

"It changes nothing."

"So, even though you love us, you can't wait for someone to come and take Bella from you. And even though you love me, you want to see me with another woman?"

"It's best for both of you." He was blind if he couldn't see that.

"That's the craziest thing I've ever heard. Why don't you let us decide what's best for us?"

"Well, what do you think, Niall? Just because we love one another that we're going to live happily ever after?"

"Well, yeah, Tammy, I do."

"I've got bad news for you, it doesn't happen that way. I'm not good at loving people. They have a tendency to leave." Her mother, her husbands.

"I think you're very good at loving people. I think you need some practice at letting people love you. Don't push me away. Don't keep me at arm's length. Let me love you."

"Niall, you're a nice man with a lot to offer. Go find yourself some nice girl to settle down with."

"I have."

"Maybe you should stop and consider your odds. My track record sucks. And being with me isn't exactly going to further your career, aside from the fact that your partner is my former father-in-law who made a pass at me. I excel at wrecking relationships. I'd rather not ruin your career as well. It's all soap opera material if I ever heard it."

"Schill isn't my partner and I still wouldn't care even if he was. And since when do you care what people say about you?"

"I don't care what they say or think about me, it's you, you addle-brained simpleton." For a smart man, he could be incredibly stupid.

"I think I'd prefer *sugar, darling, honey* or *baby* to addle-brained simpleton. Marry me, Tammy. We can have a good life together.''

She felt queasy. ''I told you from the day I met you, I'm not interested in getting married again. Ever. I don't want to be a way to heal your ego after Mia, a way to regain your pride.''

''I suppose that's fair enough. I sure as hell don't want to be the whipping boy for your ex-husbands.''

''And I'm trying to spare you that. I like living alone. It took me a long time to get to where I am—comfortable with myself in my own space. I'm not willing to risk that.''

''So, what *are* you willing to risk?''

''We could be friends.'' At this juncture it sounded lame to her.

''There's one little problem with that. Every time I'm around you I want to make love to you.''

''We could be lovers.'' She knew that was a bad idea, as well. There was no place left for either one of them to turn.

''The complication there is that every time I make love to you, it's that much harder to get up and leave. That's the problem. I want to wake up next to you in the morning, see you with a bad case of bed head and no makeup. I want forever with you.''

''Then that leaves us in love and out of luck. You talk about marriage as if a piece of paper gives you forever. All it gives you is a false sense of security. I can't do it, Niall. I can't do it to either one of us. I can't be what you want, what you need. Alone is the best way for me to be."

"There's nothing wrong with being alone. I've been alone and it's okay. Being frightened and living in that state of fear is infinitely worse, and that's what you're doing."

"So, what then? We end the same way things ended with Mia? You don't get your way, so things are over."

"I guess old habits die hard for both of us. Once again, someone gets too close to you, so you run away."

TAMMY CARRIED the day's dirty linens to the back door. For days she'd found no satisfaction or joy in her work or at home. Bella was the one bright spot. She was doing exceptionally well. In fact, Olivia would be amazed when she saw how the dog leaped about and chased the stuffed animal Tammy had bought her.

She blew out the candles in the massage room and turned off the music. She was tired. Cranky. Out of sorts. Generally miserable. And it didn't have a stinking thing to do with Niall Fortson. It didn't. She was just PMS-ing in the worst kind of way.

The bell on the front door jangled. Who the heck was this? She didn't have any other appointments and she was more than ready to go home. And Bella would be expecting her dinner soon. She pasted on a smile and walked to the waiting room.

Trena Myers stood there. Her stomach dropped.

She'd always liked Trena and had come to like her even more since they'd worked together on the dog. But Trena reminded her of Niall and, quite frankly, she didn't want to think about Niall.

"Hi, Trena. What can I do for you?"

"Hey, Tammy. I know you're closing but I thought I'd kill two birds with one stone. I need to make an appointment and I thought I'd drop by and give you the good news in person."

Tammy had begun flipping through her schedule book but paused. Her gut told her Trena's good news wouldn't necessarily be her good news. "What good news is that?"

"A greyhound rescue group contacted me today. They'll take Fair Game."

Cold dread clutched at her. "But what about the heartworms?"

"That's not a problem for them."

"But what if they can't find a home for her?"

"They're a no-kill rescue group, so she'll be okay."

"You know she's sort of different."

"I think most animals are," Trena said with a small laugh. She peered closer at Tammy. "Hey, you don't have to give her up. You can keep her. I just thought you wanted someone else to..."

"I do. That's great. When do they want her? Do they have to wait until they have room?" A few more days. Time for her to get used to the idea of Bella leaving. Maybe after Christmas.

"They can send someone the day after tomorrow to pick her up. I just need to give them a call."

That soon? The day after tomorrow? Did Niall know?

"Should I bring her to the clinic or will they pick her up from the house?"

"That's a good question. I bet they can swing by your place. That would probably be easiest. I'll call them in the morning and then give you a call. You're off on Fridays, aren't you?"

"Yeah. I should be home all morning, just let me know." Tammy stiffened her spine and forced a smile. "Now let's see when you can get in here and we'll work on your shoulder."

"I'm off next Tuesday afternoon. Do you have anything then?"

"How about one o'clock?"

"That'd be great. Dr. Fortson should be finished with his surgeries by then. He's a dream to work for. We're lucky to have him."

"He seems to be very good with the animals."

"He's awesome. Um, I know this is a sort of personal question, but are you and Dr. Fortson, you know, seeing one another?"

"I see him occasionally. He's my neighbor."

"No. I mean, like, dating him." Trena gulped a breath and rushed on without giving Tammy a chance to answer. "The times we've all worked together, I couldn't tell if...you know."

"No. We're not dating."

"He's been here three weeks and hasn't seemed interested in anyone. Do you think he might be gay?"

For the first time since their affair had ended, Tammy laughed. He was *so* not gay and he'd be mortified it had ever crossed Trena's mind. "No. I don't think he's gay."

"Whew. That would've been a waste of a good man. Well, if you're not seeing him and he's not gay, I'm going to introduce him to my sister Cecilia. I'll have her stop by the clinic one day."

Tammy had seen Cecilia in the grocery store—a perky redhead with a sweet smile. How much more wholesome could you get than a fresh-faced kindergarten teacher? "Well, there you go. Good luck with hooking your sister up with Dr. Fortson and give me a call tomorrow about the dog."

"Okay, thanks, Tammy."

"Don't mention it."

Tammy closed the door behind Trena and locked it with her shaking hand. Well, there. She'd managed to find a new home for the dog and a new woman for Niall, in one fell swoop. So why did she feel like wailing?

NIALL PUSHED himself an extra half mile on his run, welcoming the muscle strain and the drain on his energy. If he pushed himself hard enough, maybe he'd actually sleep tonight. He'd briefly thought about getting rip-roaring drunk but running seemed a better outlet.

Zoning, he ran on automatic pilot as he approached his house, his mind running through the day. He'd been double-whammied when Trena had told him Tammy'd agreed to let the rescue people pick up the dog and then added that she was setting him up with her sister.

Trena, who reminded him of Lydia with her nonstop stream of chatter, had blithely informed him that Tammy had reassured her nothing was going on between them.

So, here he was, pounding the pavement and frustrated as hell. It was one thing to realize you couldn't make someone love you. It was total hell to know someone loved you but she refused to act on it. He'd been so disappointed in Tammy, in her willingness to walk away from both him and the dog, he hadn't responded to any of Trena's pronouncements.

Wrapped in his thoughts, he didn't see the car until it was almost on him. Brakes screeched. Headlights blinded him. He jumped out of the way, the car missing him by a hairbreadth.

Niall braced his hands on his knees, his chest heaving from the run and the adrenalin surge. That had almost been really nasty.

The car door slammed and Tammy charged him. "What's wrong with you? Do you realize I almost killed you? You could be lying on the sidewalk dead right now. You can't run at night and not watch what you're doing," she yelled, semihysterical and shaking like a leaf.

He'd never heard her yell before, but then again, she'd never almost plowed him down before, either. Niall grabbed her by her shoulders. "Hey, I'm okay. You're right. I wasn't watching where I was going. But I'm okay. No harm done—except the amount of tire tread you lost when you locked it down."

"Don't joke. It's not funny. Are you hurt?"

For a week now she'd been civil yet remote. At least now she was showing real emotion. He'd take her yelling at him any day over her politely closing the door in his face.

Actually, his left leg throbbed. "I think I may have pulled a muscle jumping out of the way."

Tammy shoved her still unsteady hand through her hair. "Let me pull my car into the driveway and I'll help you."

"That's not necessary. I can make it on my own."

Tammy responded as if he hadn't even spoken. "Give me just a second."

She jumped back into the car and quickly pulled into her driveway. Niall hobbled across his yard. Tammy joined him, wrapping her arm around his waist. "Lean on me," she instructed him.

"I'm pretty sweaty."

"For God's sake, I've felt you sweaty before," she snapped.

Beneath her anger, memories of the two of them swirled between them, around them. He leaned on her. He felt her heartbeat thundering. Hell, yeah, he was willing to fight for her and he didn't mind fighting dirty.

Niall inhaled Tammy's scent, absorbed the feel of her next to him. God, he'd missed her.

Once inside the house, she started to steer him toward the sofa.

"If you wouldn't mind helping me up the stairs. I need to hit the shower." *And get you into my bed.*

"Okay. I can do that. But you're on your own with the shower."

"Of course." They'd see about that.

"Are Gigi and Memphis out back?"

"They were soaking up the last of the sun on the deck when I left for my run. Did Trena talk to you?"

"About Bella...I mean, Fair Game? Yes. She stopped by yesterday. She said a rescue group will take her tomorrow."

"You don't have to let her go," Niall argued. Somehow, he thought if he could talk her into letting the dog be a part of her life, he stood a chance with Tammy, as well.

She wouldn't look at him. "That was always the plan. We all knew I only had her on a temporary basis."

They reached his room and Niall dropped to the bed. "It's my right thigh, if you wouldn't mind taking a look at it."

"I said I would." She ran her fingers over the area. His pulled muscle didn't compare to the ache that suffused the rest of him.

Running shorts didn't hide his burgeoning erection. Tammy's face flushed and her touch changed to a more sensuous stroke. He'd counted on her not being able to resist him any more than he could resist her.

"Does it hurt?" she asked, her breath uneven.

"It hurts real bad. I was hoping you could do something for it."

"An ice pack would help."

"That wasn't what I had in mind. I was thinking wet heat would be more effective." He pulled his sweatshirt off and dropped it on the floor beside the bed.

"Niall," she protested. Her eyes had that hot, glittery look he loved.

Oh, yeah, he was starting to get to her. And it wasn't a one-way street. He was hard as a rock for her.

"You said you'd felt me sweaty before. You've seen me like this before." He shrugged. "Could you help me with my shoes before you go? They're laced pretty tight."

"No problem." She knelt at his feet and fumbled with the laces.

"Take your time."

She glanced up and had to look past Mount Rushmore. She wet her lower lip with her tongue and he pulsed against the tented nylon. "Oh. My." Her fingers tangled in the laces and pulled them tighter.

"I think I have a fever."

"You've got a pulled muscle. It doesn't give you a fever."

"Well, something has. And you offered to take care

of me. You should check because I'm very hot right now."

"Cold compresses work well on a fever."

"Not the kind I have. Cold showers sure haven't done a thing for it. Come here, Tammy. Touch me and tell me if I'm hot."

She started to put her hand against his forehead and he caught her wrist. "No. The best place to check for a fever is the stomach."

He placed her hand on his belly, just above the elastic waistband of his shorts and his jutting hard-on. "What do you want, Niall?"

Everything. You. He looked at her and let her see it in his eyes, on his face, the love he felt for her, the way she completed him. She could leave if she couldn't handle it. But if she stayed, he wanted her to know love was there. In him. Between them. "Touch me."

She slid her hand beneath his waistband and ran her fingers along his length.

"Taste me."

She pushed his shorts down, easing them over his erection. She tugged them off and threw them to the floor. Her clothes quickly followed his.

She knelt on the bed beside him and started to bend forward. "Wait," he said.

He grasped her thigh and pulled her across him, until she straddled his shoulders, facing south, her sex quivering before him, the heady scent of her arousal surrounding him.

Holding her hips with his hands, he leaned forward

and swiped his tongue along her glistening valley. Her moan reverberated against his tip as she encased his length in her hot, wet mouth.

"Let the feasting begin."

13

"I AM RUNNING out of patience." Olivia stormed through the door and slammed it behind her.

Hadn't she ever heard of knocking?

"Go away." Tammy didn't bother to ask how Olivia knew the dog was gone. There were no secrets in Colthersville. Tammy blew her nose on a soggy tissue and buried her face in a striped silk pillow. She'd probably ruined the pillow. She didn't care. "This doesn't concern you and I want to be alone."

Olivia planted herself in front of the sofa, hands on her hips, bristling with attitude. "So sad, too bad."

"Don't you have anything else to do?"

"As a matter of fact, I've got a ton of stuff to do. I've got a couple of more presents to buy, decorations to get up for the library Christmas party tomorrow night, and I have to go to the grocery store so I can prepare Christmas dinner for my crazy, dysfunctional family in a few days. But I've got to prioritize and right now I've got to knock some sense into you, first."

Tammy was not up for this. The dog had been gone for two hours and she still felt raw and bleeding. "It's my life, Olivia."

"Ye-ah. And you are making a royal mess of it."

"I've been doing that for thirty-two years, so why all the concern now?"

Olivia handed her a fresh tissue. "The pity party ends now. Suck it up and turn on your brain." Olivia threw her hands up in the air. "I swear. We Cooper sisters are a mess. I came this close—" she almost touched her forefinger to her thumb "—to walking away from Luke. And he's, without a doubt, the best thing that's ever happened to me. I try not to think about how close I came to ruining my life. So, there is no way I'm going to stand by and watch you do something stupid like let Niall and that dog go."

Olivia only paused a second to catch her breath. Even if Tammy had a comment to make, she couldn't have squeezed it in. Olivia plopped down on the sofa beside her.

"Your other husbands were takers, Tammy. They wanted you. They wanted you to love them, wait on them, blow their minds with sex. But they didn't have anything to give. And whether you realized it or not, you wouldn't let them give you anything, anyway, because you wouldn't let them get that close. It was so obvious that night at dinner and then when you and Niall brought Bella out to the farm for a run—the man is so in love with you he can hardly see straight. And yes, he wants to take, but he also wants to give you back as much as he takes, or more. That's what makes him different from the other men in your life and that's the part you can't handle. The way he looked at you the first time I met him at your house—" she rubbed her arms "—it still gives me chills. I knew he was Mr. Right."

"I've worked so hard to get where I am."

"I know you have. I'm proud of you and no one's asking you to give that up. Tammy, you were still looking for *you* when you married Jerry, Allen and Earl. They tried to make you into what they wanted you to be and you let them, because you didn't know who you were. You've grown so much. You know who you are now, or at least you've got a good idea. You're not looking for yourself in Niall. You've found you and that's who he loves."

Olivia made it all sound so easy, but Tammy couldn't trust any of it. "I do love him. I love him enough to stay away from him. He'll find someone else. I can't stand to sit by and watch him fall out of love with me."

"First of all, he's not going to find someone else. He doesn't want anyone else. That's plain enough to see. Second, he's not gonna fall out of love with you, not if you can actually learn to let him love you, and I think you can. Third, how would you feel if I told you Bella slipped her leash and got hit by a car and Niall got hurt trying to save her?"

For infinitesimal moments, her heart stopped. No blood flowed through her veins. Her stomach clenched. The bottom dropped out of her world and she felt herself free-fall through a dark, cold void. She reined herself back. *If.* Olivia had said *if.* "I would say you were immeasurably cruel to do that."

Olivia appeared totally unrepentant. "No, the true cruelty would be if that happened without you, Niall and Bella having lived every day to the fullest together."

And the truth in that nauseated her, as well.

TRENA STUCK her head in the door of Niall's office. "That's it for the day, Doc. You need anything else before I go?"

Niall climbed out on a limb and asked the question that had hovered on his tongue the entire day. "Did that greyhound rescue group pick up Fair Game today?"

"They sure did. Picked her up this morning. She's such a sweetie, I predict she'll have a new home in no time."

Niall's heart sank and his stomach bottomed out. There hadn't been a thing wrong with the home she'd found except the stubborn, insecure woman who lived there.

He wouldn't let her do it. She'd distanced herself and people had let her. By God, he wasn't going to let her get away with it. He didn't need for her to marry him. He didn't need for her to move in. He just needed her to give them a chance. She loved him and she loved that dog and the two of them would wait a lifetime for her if that's what it took. Of course, he was hoping it didn't take nearly that long.

"Can you get me the phone number for the rescue group before you go?" he asked.

"Sure thing."

Trena returned within a minute and handed him a slip with the number and a contact name. Curiosity was written all over her face.

"I'm going to adopt Fair Game," Niall told her. "She's small-animal friendly—I tested her with Olivia's cat when we took her to run at their farm—so she should get along with my crew just fine."

A huge grin spread over Trena's face. "That is very, very cool." She shifted from foot to foot.

"Was there something else?"

"Max and I are having a little Christmas party tomorrow night and I was hoping you'd come."

Niall had met Trena's husband and liked him. And Niall thought the world of Trena. The more he was around her at work, the more she reminded him of Lydia. "Sure."

"Great. My sister will be there, as well. I'd like for you to meet her."

That had setup written all over it. He'd been too stunned to say anything the other day, but not now. The only decent course of action was to set the record straight. "You're one of the nicest people I've met in Colthersville and I'm sure your sister is just as nice and just as pretty as you are, but it wouldn't be fair for me to meet her."

"Oh, God, you're gay." She clapped her hand over her mouth, horrified. "I didn't mean to say that."

"Gay?" Niall leaned back in his chair and roared. He laughed until tears ran down his face, overreacting but desperately needing the physical outlet. He finally wiped his eyes and composed himself. Trena remained stricken. "No. I hate to disappoint you, but I'm a heterosexual."

"Oh, geez, I hope you're not gonna fire me over this. I really didn't mean to say it. It just slipped out."

Man, did she remind him of Lydia.

"Your job's safe. No one's fired. But I'd really appreciate it if you didn't share the gay theory with anyone else."

"Sure thing." She looked marginally relieved.

"For the record, I am totally, absolutely, out-of-my-mind in love with Tammy. And I expect to stay this way for a long time. The rest of my life, in fact. So you can see why it wouldn't be fair for me to meet your sister if she's interested in any kind of a relationship."

Trena mouth hung open, at a loss for words. A novel experience, he'd wager.

"Are you okay?" he asked.

"But she said...you weren't...she didn't...I'd never have asked..."

"Tammy's got some issues she has to work through, but we're gonna get there." If she didn't kill him first for telling Trena, which was essentially making an announcement to the world in general.

She pulled herself together, another one of those grins blossoming across her freckled face. She leaned across his desk and high-fived him. "You go, Doc."

"Want to hang around, while I call on the new dog for Tammy and me?" he asked with an answering grin. It felt damn good to tell Trena he loved Tammy. Hell, he'd tell anyone who'd listen. He was mounting an all-out, no-holds-barred offensive. He might've lost a few battles, but dammit, he was going to win the war.

A woman answered on the second ring and he identified himself and told her why he was calling. And then she knocked the wind right out of his sails.

"But she can't already be adopted," he protested. "You just got her this morning."

"I'm sorry, Dr. Fortson, but she has been. Catherine's handling Fair Game's case and she settled it about an hour ago. Actually closer to forty-five minutes."

Forty-five minutes. Forty-five minutes too late. "Can I speak to Catherine?"

"She's gone for the day and she took the file with her so she could fill out the paperwork and get it ready. The new owner's picking her up tomorrow morning."

Niall was desperate. "Listen, I'll pay twice the

adoption fee, if you can talk the other owner out of the dog. Make it triple."

"Dr. Fortson, I know you're disappointed, but you know we can't do that," the voice on the other end gently chided him. "We have several other nice dogs that you could come by and meet."

"I don't want another dog. I want that dog." Bravo. He sounded like a three-year-old throwing a temper tantrum. "I'm sorry. It's just that Fair Game's special."

"I understand. I really do. It's terribly disappointing, but Catherine said the adoption was a Christmas gift, so I really don't see them changing their mind. I'm sorry."

"Thank you for your help."

"Merry Christmas," she said.

"Merry Christmas to you, too."

Trena shook her head when he hung up the phone. "It's okay, Doc. She'll love you with or without the dog."

Niall wished he felt as sure as she sounded. And it didn't change the fact that he loved the dog as much as Tammy did. "Cancel my appointments for tomorrow morning. I'm going to talk someone out of a dog tomorrow."

TAMMY PARKED her car in the auto parts parking lot and stuck her keys under the mat. She climbed into the big truck with the 4X4 tires and three inch lift. Sure enough, the keys were in the glove box, exactly where Marty said he'd leave them.

She and her brother weren't particularly close, but he usually came through in a pinch. And it didn't hurt that it was Christmas. Marty loved his truck. She wasn't so sure he'd have loaned it to her in January.

She backed out and followed the directions she'd scribbled on a piece of paper out of town. She'd driven along Barn Owl Road hundreds of times but it looked totally different sitting up high in the truck instead of low to the ground in her little car. Same view. Different perspective.

That's what Olivia had given her yesterday, a different perspective. And a healthy dose of backbone. Tammy had once told Niall regret was a waste of time, and she'd meant it. But she'd realized that she'd been living around the edges of life, afraid to jump in with two feet, and that wasted more than time. Sure, she could go along, keeping herself emotionally distant, safe, but what was the point? And that also included the arrogant assumption that she could guard her heart. Yet another fallacy. Somehow Niall and Bella had slipped past the guard and stolen her heart.

Olivia had shaken her up. Life was a one-shot deal, not a dress rehearsal. She was going to live it to the fullest and that included heartache and pain and loss but it included joy and happiness, as well. One didn't come without the other.

More content than she'd ever been in her life,

Tammy drove down the highway, singing Christmas songs along with the radio, the heater cranked and the window down so the cold wind whipped through her hair. Happiness stole through her, growing stronger moment by moment, chasing away the fear.

She belted out the final verse of "Santa Claus Is Coming to Town" as she pulled up in front of the green metal building. A couple of cars sat in the parking lot. A sign by the metal front door proclaimed this was the Southern Regional Greyhound Adoption Agency. Her hands shook with excitement as she pocketed the truck keys and climbed out.

SRGAA opened at 9:00 a.m. It was 9:01. Tammy walked into a small room with a worn metal desk and a couple of chairs. Barking and rooing echoed from the interior. Adoption forms and a tub of stuffed dog toys sat on a folding table against one wall. A door led to another room.

A short woman with a gracious smile and kind eyes emerged from the other room. "Hi, I'm Catherine. You must be Tammy."

Tammy shook her hand, "Yes. It's nice to meet you." She peered past Catherine to the room beyond. She'd missed Bella terribly in the twenty-four hours she'd been gone. "Can I see Bella...uh, Fair Game?"

"Go ahead and call her Bella. She's yours." Catherine smiled. "Sure. Come on back. She's in the first set of kennels off the adoption office. And I have the paperwork all filled out. Usually there's a seven-day waiting period but since you were fostering her already it'll just take us a few minutes and then you'll be on your way."

Tammy followed Catherine from the waiting room, through the adoption area—another desk and a couple of chairs—to the kennel area. Six chainlink stalls lined a wall. Each stall held a greyhound. All of them stood. A few barked.

Bella, in a middle stall, began to jump and bark, her long whip of a tail lashing furiously against the chain link. "Hi, sweetheart," Tammy crooned. "There's my girl. Let me fill out this paperwork and I'll take you home. I've missed you so much." She swiped away a few tears.

"I'd say she's glad to see her mom." Catherine smiled indulgently.

"I missed her." Tammy looked at the row of narrow, elegant faces lined up on either side of Bella and her heart ached. "I hate it that they'll spend Christmas here. I wish I could take them all."

"Someone will come over twice on Christmas Day to check on them. I'll be over at least once. They'll all find homes eventually, and we'll keep them until they do. We're a 'no kill' group, so relax, all these guys are going to be okay." Catherine herded her back to a chair in the middle office. "Let's take care of this paperwork."

Catherine sat down on the opposite side of the desk. Just as she pulled out the paperwork, the outer door opened and the buzzer announced a new visitor. "If you want to read through these forms, I'll be right back." Catherine excused herself.

Caught up in the excitement and the paperwork, Tammy tuned out the other room—until the voice filtered through. She knew that deep baritone. Niall. A thousand butterflies fluttered in her belly, and her blood rushed to her head, leaving her light-headed. This would be a really lousy time to faint.

From where she sat, she couldn't see beyond the doorway. But she could hear and she listened shamelessly.

Niall introduced himself to Catherine, explaining he'd been the vet in charge of Fair Game. "I called last night but you'd already gone. I know you've found someone to adopt her, but is there any way you can work with me on this? I've grown very attached to her and someone I care about very much loves Fair Game. I'll pay extra. Please," he pleaded, desperation evident in his voice.

How could she have ever doubted this wonderful, sweet man who'd go to such lengths to bring her back the dog she'd been so stupid to let go in the first place? Tears flowed unchecked down her face, as if a dam had burst inside her. Tammy jumped to her feet and flew across the room.

"I think—" Catherine began.

Tammy launched herself past Catherine and into Niall's arms. She took full advantage of his surprise, bracketing his face in her hands and kissing him with every ounce of apology and promise she could muster. Once his initial shock wore off, he kissed her back. It was heaven in his arms, tasting him, feeling his body against hers.

"I see you've met." Catherine's wry observation ended their kiss. Niall lifted his head but kept his arms around her. It'd take a dynamite blast to move her. "I'm going to take a wild guess you're the one he wants Fair Game for," Catherine said.

"She's the one," Niall said with that smile, the one that made her weak-kneed. Good thing he had a tight grip on her. He looked down at Tammy, "Where's your car?"

"I borrowed my brother's truck so I could fit the crate," Tammy said.

Trena popped around from behind Niall and waved at Tammy. Tammy hadn't even noticed her, she'd been so focused on Niall. "I came along for moral support," Trena explained. She looked at Catherine. "He's buggy about her. He proclaimed his deep and abiding love for her yesterday afternoon. It was very touching."

Tammy gasped. Niall was running around telling people he loved her? That didn't strike her as a wise move for the new vet in town. But it was terribly romantic. "You didn't."

His wicked smile started in his eyes. "I did."

"Ya'll better settle this thing, because he was talking

about some crazy billboard scheme on the way over here. Tammy, talk some sense into him before everyone on Highway 109 sees *I love you, Tammy. Signed, Niall* in ten-foot letters on the way into town."

"You wouldn't." Her heart pounded so hard she could barely breathe.

"I would," he vowed. He traced his thumb against her cheek, regardless of their audience. "I'm prepared to spend a lifetime convincing you I love you."

"Come on. I'll fill you in." Tammy vaguely registered Trena grabbing Catherine's arm, pulling her into the other room, and closing the door.

"Bella and I were going to surprise you this afternoon."

"You beat me to the punch." He chuckled. "Bella and I were going to surprise you on Christmas Day." His caramel-flecked eyes grew serious and he smoothed her hair behind her ear. "I love you, Tammy. I'll always love you. If you don't want to get married, I don't need that piece of paper. I just need to know we have a future together. We can be the talk of the town. Some couples have his and her bathrooms. We can have his and her houses." His grin melted her from the inside out.

"I love you, you crazy, romantic man. And I love the idea of his and her houses, with a gate between our backyards. Maybe, in a couple of years, when we start a family, we can think about looking at one house."

"A family?" He looked a little excited and a whole lot nervous.

She definitely related. "We won't rush anything." She nuzzled the tempting space beneath his jaw. He was solid, warm and incredibly sexy. And, oh yeah, he was hers. "You've wrecked my Christmas present. Now I've got to get you something else."

"I'm sure something will come up." He rocked against her and a delicious warmth spread through her.

Something was coming up all right. She rocked back.

"Behave," they admonished one another simultaneously.

Niall laughed and pulled her hips closer. "Well, maybe don't behave too much."

Tammy curled her leg around his, nestling him closer, harder between her thighs. "How about barely behaving?"

Niall groaned his approval. "Let's get our dog and go home. You can give me my Christmas present early. I know just what I want."

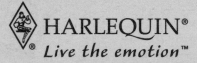

HARLEQUIN® *Blaze*™

HARLEQUIN® *Temptation*®

Single in South Beach

Nightlife on the Strip just got a little hotter!

Join author Joanne Rock as she takes you to Miami Beach and its hottest new singles playground. Club Paradise has opened for business and the women in charge are determined to succeed at all costs. So what will they do with the sexy men who show up at the club?

SEX & THE SINGLE GIRL
Harlequin Blaze #104
September 2003

GIRL'S GUIDE TO HUNTING & KISSING
Harlequin Blaze #108
October 2003

ONE NAUGHTY NIGHT
Harlequin Temptation #951
November 2003

Don't miss these red-hot stories from Joanne Rock!
Watch for the sizzling nightlife to continue in spring 2004.

Look for these books at your favorite retail outlet.

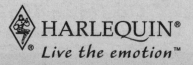

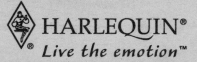